THEY CALLED HIM A DRIFTER—
A FIDDLEFOOT

But Frank Chess wasn't a weakling. He just never cared enough about anything to fight for it. So nobody ever realized what could happen when Frank stumbled over a cause that really mattered to him.

Right then, Frank Chess was through running away. He was ready to explode into a killing rage and destroy everything that stood against him. He was no longer the soft, mild-mannered FIDDLEFOOT. He was a tornado of vengeance.

Books by Luke Short

- THE FEUD AT SINGLE SHOT
- RAIDERS OF THE RIMROCK
- WAR ON THE CIMARRON
- SUNSET GRAZE
- AND THE WIND BLOWS FREE
- CORONER CREEK
- RIDE THE MAN DOWN
- HIGH VERMILION
- STATION WEST
- VENGEANCE VALLEY
- SADDLE BY STARLIGHT
- PLAY A LONE HAND
- SILVER ROCK
- RIMROCK
- THE WHIP
- SUMMER OF THE SMOKE
- GUNMAN'S CHANCE
- LAST HUNT
- KING COLT
- DEAD FREIGHT FOR PIUTE
- THE SOME-DAY COUNTRY
- THE MAN ON THE BLUE
- AMBUSH
- FIRST CAMPAIGN
- HARDCASE
- FIRST CLAIM
- DESERT CROSSING
- FIDDLEFOOT

Published by Bantam Books

LUKE SHORT

FIDDLEFOOT

BANTAM BOOKS · TORONTO · NEW YORK · LONDON

FIDDLEFOOT

A Bantam Book

PRINTING HISTORY

Serialized in SATURDAY EVENING POST *March-April 1946*
Houghton Mifflin edition published April 1949
Bantam edition published January 1951
2nd printing ......January 1951
3rd printing ....July 1951
4th printing ....November 1952
New Bantam edition published April 1958
2nd printing ....April 1965

*Bantam Books are published by Bantam Books, Inc., a subsidiary
of Grosset & Dunlap, Inc. Its trade-mark, consisting of the words
"Bantam Books" and the portrayal of a bantam, is registered in the
United States Patent Office and in other countries. Marca Registrada.
Bantam Books, Inc., 271 Madison Avenue, New York, N. Y. 10016.*

FIDDLEFOOT

Chapter 1

I T WAS UP ABOVE in the mountain meadows and the aspens that Roan Creek found and spent its first vigor. Here below, in the wedge of dark canyon, it prowled quietly around vast boulders under the black shade of the pines, patient enough now to form deep and sunless pools.

The young man in the dusty blue uniform of a second lieutenant, United States Cavalry, lay on his belly atop a flat high boulder, and he was watching one of these pools. His arms were folded on the boulder's edge, and his chin was cushioned on his arms. His black campaign hat lay beside him, and a faint checkering of early morning sunlight touched his right leg and scuffed cavalry boots. His long form was motionless, relaxed, as if he had been here some time.

He watched the water at the base of this boulder for many minutes, then rolled over on his side and from his hip pocket drew a crumpled, non-regulation red-checked bandanna handkerchief. Putting a corner of it in his mouth, he tore the hem with his teeth, and then, with strong sun-blackened hands, he ripped off the corner. Wadding up this piece, he put it in his mouth and when it was wet he took it out and balled it between his fingers, then rolled back on his belly. With his right hand, he made a couple of practice passes, and then threw the wad of handkerchief into the pool. It landed at the base of the boulder opposite, and then, caught by the slow current, unfurled gradually in the dark water, a patch of brilliant color.

Deep in the pool at the base of the boulder something moved. The young man watched intently while a dark uncertain shape

1

detached itself from the black rock and was finally outlined against the lighter-colored gravel of the pool's bottom. It was a trout, thick as a man's calf and as long as his arm. Motionless now, it lifted warily toward the patch of color. Then, its curiosity satisfied, it halted, suspending itself a bare moment before it circled majestically against the current and vanished under the ledge.

Frank Chess rose to his feet now and picked up his campaign hat. He was a tall young man, slow-moving now in abstraction, and he looked briefly again at the pool, a lingering soberness in his dark eyes. The expression went oddly with his face, which was narrow and dark and held an indefinable hint of cheerfulness and even impudence, now overlaid with thoughtfulness.

He clambered off the high boulder and began the steep climb up through the thick pines. Once, just below the rim, he turned to look back and saw through a break in the trees, the dark, silent pool. The bit of handkerchief was gone.

His horse was tethered in the timber beyond the rim, and he stepped into the McClellan saddle, cut over the ridge, and presently picked up a cattle trail which brought him in another hour to a dim road. He traveled this only a short way, left it again for timber, and by noon reached an obscure canyon where he picked up a faint wagon road. In a short while, he came to a clearing where a sorry looking tangle of corrals huddled close to a rotting shack.

The man who was standing in the door of the shack now leaned his rifle against the inside wall and stepped out into the sunlight. He was an unshaven, middle-aged man in tattered denims and rundown half-boots, but there was a genuine pleasure in his slack face now as he grinned and said, "Hello, Frank. Didn't figure to see you for two-three weeks yet. Where's the bunch?"

"Coming, Ed," Frank said, and then he added, "Rob's dead." He stepped out of the saddle, took off his hat, and slapped the dust from his trousers. Looking up now, he caught the slack-mouthed amazement in Ed Hanley's face.

"Well, well," Ed said then. "I always figured Rob was too mean to die."

Frank said, "Hide that horse and get mine, will you?" and went on into the shack.

When he came out some minutes later, he was wearing a faded calico shirt, worn denim pants, and scuffed cowman's boots. Ed led a saddled sorrel gelding from the corrals, and Frank accepted the reins in silence and mounted.

"Need anything?" Frank asked.

Ed scratched his head. "Nothin' but company." Now he looked carefully up at Frank and said slyly, "Maybe somethin' else too."

"What?"

"You're a rich man now, ain't you?" Ed asked softly. "I need money."

Frank looked at him a long moment, and then swung his leg over the saddle and dismounted. He walked up to Hanley and hit him in the face, hard.

Hanley sprawled on his back on the dust. After shaking his head once, he rose. Frank hit him again in the face, and again Hanley went down. This time, he rolled over on an elbow and he and Frank watched each other a long, long moment.

"Still need it?" Frank asked quietly.

"I don't reckon."

Frank stepped into the saddle and rode out of the clearing without looking back.

It was almost dark when he reached the switchbacks above the town of Rifle and the last ridge before Grand River's gorge. The two-score false-front frame buildings making up the town's business district fronted both sides of the road, and this road crossed the narrow bench paralleling the river. Lamps were being lighted now against the August dusk, and from this height Frank could hear the whoops of the kids playing along the river after the supper hour. Immediately below him, the big spread of high-country pine that laced the residence part of the town was black and murmuring with the breeze of coming night.

At the bottom of the grade, he turned downriver, avoiding the main street. There, across the road and past the last mean shack on the town's outskirts, was a narrow frame building set beside a high gate which bore the legend on the boards of its wide arch:

J. J. HULST

Horses Bought and Sold

A high board fence began at the open gate and ran several hundred gray and sagging feet toward town, and behind it the big barns and sheds and corrals were scattered in an orderly maze clear to the river-bank. The rich and not unpleasant smell of manure was in the air like a stain.

The office was lighted, and Frank rode under the arch, dismounted and tied his horse out of the drive. Back across the corrals he could see the dim flicker of the stable lanterns.

Mounting the short steps to the open side door leading into the front office, he went in and glanced around at the three slanting desks behind the rail. This was a shabby room, and he was moving purposefully through it toward the door in its rear wall when he remarked the lamps still burning there, and remembered Tess Falette.

He halted suddenly and looked about him, and he saw her kneeling in front of the safe, putting away some ledgers. When she heard his footsteps pause, she looked over her shoulder. There was faint irritation in her face that vanished immediately at sight of him; she rose, a long-legged, slim and shining girl, softly rounded under her dark office dress that exaggerated her pale and gleaming hair, and she lent a kind of splendor to this drab room. Her dark eyes held warm and honest greeting for him as he came over to the rail.

"You're working too late, Tess," he said, in a tone without banter.

"Why are teamsters always drunk when they unload?" she asked him. Her voice was low and husky, and it held an admission of the deep pleasure she felt now as she said, "It's nice you're back, Frank." She smiled, meaning it, and Frank read the gay spirit of her in her smile. Her mouth was wide and sweetly shaped, her eyes set wide apart, and in them now was a lingering and friendly appraisal of him, as if, since they had talked only a few times and briefly in the three months he had worked for Hulst, she was still learning about him, and at the same time liking him.

He said, "Back for good this time," and because this reminded him of his errand, he asked, "Rhino still in, Tess?"

She nodded, and he smiled at her and moved on through the door into a hall. Down it a dozen feet, lamplight was pooled in front of an open door, and he walked through it.

The man sitting at the roll-top desk had heard him and was waiting. He was a tall man going to fat, immensely big-framed, and a kind of bull-like vitality was reflected in his ruddy face, which held a curious benignity. He had close-cropped white hair that lay rich and shining close to his round skull, and there was a tranquil shrewdness in his bleak eyes as he beheld Frank. His worn vest lacked inches of meeting across his high belly, and the rest of his clothes were mussed and careless, and utterly clean. He lifted a big hand about four inches off the desk in lazy greeting and said, "Hello, Boy," and Frank said quietly, "Hello, Rhino," and sank into the chair against the near wall.

Rhino surveyed him a moment in silence, and then said gently, "I got word to you as soon as I could, Frank. I'm sorry about Rob."

Frank said idly, "You don't care a damn, Rhino, and you know it."

Rhino Hulst eyed him without rancor and then smiled faintly. "All right, I don't. No more than you."

Frank made no protest. The unaccustomed soberness still lingered in his face; he stretched his feet before him and pushed his worn Stetson to the back of his head. His hatband had pressed down his short curly brown hair at the temples. He ran a hand idly through his hair.

"Where'd Dick find you?" Rhino asked.

"Northern Utah." Frank sat up, putting his elbows on the arms of his chair, and looking now at the big man, asked, "Now tell me."

"Dick told you all I know. Fred Dutra was bringing some cattle over Battle Mountain Pass. They spooked away from something on the trail where it rounded the peak. He found Rob lying just off the trail." Rhino's massive hand was lying palm down on the desk; he turned it over, shrugged his shoulders an eighth of an inch and pursed his lips. "He'd fallen and broken his back. Weeks ago, Fred said. They buried him yesterday."

Frank settled slowly back in his chair again, looking deliberately about this dismal hot cubbyhole of an office. A faint distaste was reflected in his face as he drew a sack of tobacco dust from his shirt pocket and carefully rolled a cigarette, concentrating on it. He finished it, touched a match to it, and looking over its flame he saw Rhino eyeing him with a bland and bored patience.

Wake him up, he thought and flipped the match to the floor and said, "I'm quitting, Rhino."

Rhino nodded once, unperturbed.

"You'll have to get someone else in your bunch to wear that soldier suit—somebody that won't get hog-drunk in public. You got anybody like that, Rhino?"

The big man was silent a moment, curiosity in his pale eyes now. "You're mad, Frank," he said then.

Frank said nothing.

"Mad at being left almost rich?" Rhino asked gently. "Or mad at losing a stepfather you hated and that hated you?" Rhino's eyes narrowed shrewdly. "It couldn't be remorse, could it, Frank? You didn't treat him well."

"No," Frank said quietly. "I'm glad he's dead."

"You should be," Rhino murmured, in lazy contempt. "You still won't have to work, now you've got Saber. That's a big ranch. It'll take you a long time to go through all that money."

"Now who's mad?" Frank asked dryly.

Rhino shook his head. "No, you're wrong, Frank. I don't begrudge you Saber. I don't begrudge you anything. You know why?"

"Tell me," Frank said mockingly.

Rhino smiled meagerly. "You'll lose it. You aren't man enough to hold it. You won't ever marry Carrie Tavister and settle down. You'll get fiddlefooted again, and you'll want to drift. Saber will go through your fingers like so much sand, and you'll be off to Oregon or Mexico. But you'll be back."

"And beg you for the soldier suit?" Frank asked dryly.

The flush on Rhino's face deepened imperceptibly. "You'll want it, but you won't get it."

Frank shook his head. "No, I'll never want to wear it again, Rhino. I never liked to wear it."

"Naturally," Rhino said with open malice. "It took some nerve. I'm surprised you ever wore it."

"So am I," Frank said calmly.

Rhino's eyebrows lifted. "You admit it?"

Frank nodded. "Yes. Every time I'd go into a town and announce I was an officer buying horses for the cavalry, I expected someone to ask me for my credentials. Every time I rejected a good horse worth a hundred and twenty-five dollars, I expected a rancher to make me prove the phony reasons I gave him. And every time Hugh Nunnally stepped out of the crowd and offered the seller forty dollars for the horse, I expected to be mobbed. I'll never know why those ranchers never connected me with Hugh—or both of us with you."

"You're quite a hero," Rhino said.

"Yes," Frank said quietly. They looked at each other levelly, and a slow puzzlement came into Rhino's face.

"What did you come here for?" he asked.

"To tell you that. I'm a poor crook, Rhino. I don't like it. I'm quitting." He leaned forward, and repeated, "I'm quitting."

"I heard you," Rhino said. He regarded Frank a long time and then observed dryly, "You think it's that easy?"

Frank carefully dropped his cigarette on the floor and ground it out. He said, almost idly, "When Ed Hanley heard Rob was dead, he said he needed money."

Rhino turned this over in his mind, and smiled.

"I hit him. He changed his mind."

Rhino still smiled, and Frank stood up.

"Walk soft, Rhino," he murmured, and when Rhino didn't answer, he went out.

The office was dark and empty as he went through it; he got his horse and rode out the gate, turning toward town. It puzzled him obscurely that Rhino's words had the power to rankle. He had expected no less because this was Rhino's fair opinion of him, which, in turn, was the town's opinion also. *And with the bark on, it's Carrie's, too,* he reflected. You couldn't drift over a dozen states for five years to come home and expect people to do more than laugh at your stories while they bitterly envied you. Nor should you have one of the biggest ranches in the country given you as a reward for that idleness. He shifted in the saddle, pondering this now, as he had pondered it these last four days coming from Utah. There was Carrie to see tonight, and he shrank from that, for the reward he had received for his irresponsibility was also a reward for five years of neglect of her. There was a name for him, he understood now, and Rhino had named him. He was a fiddlefoot.

Ahead of him now, he saw a figure vaguely outlined against

the town's light walking in the road, and presently, overtaking it, he saw it was Tess Falette. She was bareheaded, carrying her hat, and she was humming a soft tune in the night.

He drew alongside her and, touching his hat, said, "You too old to ride double, Tess?"

Her laugh was warm, and she said, "Not too old, Frank, but I'd rather walk. I sit down too much."

The distaste for the hour ahead of him prompted Frank now to step out of the saddle and fall in beside this girl, leading his horse.

They were silent for a minute, both a little surprised and pleased at his action, and the silence began to dim the sharpness of Rhino's words.

Tess said pleasantly now, "What's that country like where you were?"

"A big white dry bone, some of it."

He heard her sigh. "I started out to see it once when I was twelve. My dad brought me back, because little girls didn't run away, he said." Her warm laugh came again, and he found himself carefully recalling what he knew of this girl. In the three months he had worked for Rhino, he had come in from buying trips only rarely and at hours that sometimes made him miss her entirely. He recalled someone saying she was a daughter of one of Rhino's former teamsters who had died, and that Rhino had given over to her the running of his trifling freighting business.

Now she said, "How far did you go?"

"Almost into Idaho."

"Did you men stick together or did you split up?" Tess asked. Frank looked down at her in the dark, a caution touching him now. Most certainly, this girl was not in on any of Rhino's dozen secretive schemes, and he was wary of her curiosity.

"We split up. That's a big country."

"Were you alone any of the time?"

Frank halted in the road now, and she halted too, facing him. "I know I'm snooping, Frank," she said quietly, forestalling him. "I'll tell you in a minute. Will you answer me?"

"No, I wasn't alone," Frank lied.

"And you can prove it?"

"By Hugh Nunnally. But why should I prove it?"

Tess turned now, saying, "So Rhino didn't tell you?"

Frank said nothing, and fell in beside her, and presently Tess said, "Buck Hannan's been in the office three times this week since they found your stepfather."

"He's sheriff. Why not?"

"He keeps asking if you've come in yet."

Frank put out a hand now, and Tess halted, and Frank said in a low voice, "What are you trying to tell me, Tess?"

"Your stepfather had been dead two or three weeks before he was found."

"So Rhino said."

"You've been gone how long—two months?"

"A month and a half this time."

"You and your stepfather had had a quarrel, and that news is all over town, Frank."

"We had a lot of quarrels," Frank said grimly. "A thousand, maybe."

"Yes, but you own Saber, now he's dead. That might mean something to Hannan."

Frank was utterly still a moment. "That means Hannan thinks Rob was murdered."

"And that you might have done it."

Frank let his hand drop from Tess's arm, and they began walking again. It was odd that Rhino hadn't told him this. As for Rob being murdered, the fact was of complete indifference to him, and of little curiosity. It had been years since he had felt anything about Rob Custis save a quiet and controlled hatred. So many people felt the same way that he had always accepted it as inevitable that Rob would die a violent death.

They were on the outskirts of town now and a couple of Slash H riders overtook them and spoke quietly to Frank. Where the first tie-rail of the business section and its boardwalk began, Frank halted. A few of the stores were still open, their lamps casting a faint glow over the quiet main street. By their light, Frank regarded the girl beside him, and he surprised her watching him with an expression of gravity that was mingled with curiosity.

"Where do you live, Tess?"

"I have a room at the hotel."

He spoke slowly now. "Thanks for telling me this. But why did you?"

The faintest of smiles curled a corner of her wide, full mouth. "Maybe because you've never asked me to take a buggy ride in the moonlight." She shrugged. "Maybe I like a man who laughs once in a while. Maybe I don't think it's a crime to be fiddle-footed. I don't know, Frank. Good night."

He touched his hat and watched her move off down the boardwalk, still carrying her hat in her hand, a straight girl with a proud walk. A faint curiosity stirred within him as he watched her, and for a moment his face lost its unaccustomed soberness, and then he turned and stepped into the saddle.

Chapter 2

TAVISTER'S HOUSE was a high, two-story affair set on a corner behind a deep lawn, and from the porch chair where Carrie sat in the darkness now, the sounds of the main street two blocks away were distant and muffled. She heard her father prowling about his study upstairs; a buggy passed on the street, the hoofbeats of the horse muffled in the thick summer dust, and after that it was quiet.

Too quiet, Carrie thought dismally. After five years of waiting, she should have learned to curb her impatience, but she never had. The mere knowledge that word had been sent to Frank had brought her out here for the last three nights. If her pride allowed it, she knew she would have been waiting at the stepping block—as close to him, she thought wryly, as she could get.

The pots of geraniums strung along the front steps had ceased gurgling and bubbling from the water she had already given them, and now she leaned down for the watering can beside her to give them more. This was a ritual in the summer, so old its origin was lost in childhood. Three times a week, all the pots of flowers in the house were brought out, lined along the steps, and thoroughly drenched.

She was bent over, fumbling for the can in the darkness of

the porch, when she heard the hoofbeats. Rising quickly, she saw the dim shape of a rider come even with the walk, pass the stepping block, and dismount.

A feeling of excitement almost choked her, but she remained where she was. At last, by the dim lamplight of the hall shining through the front door, she saw him, tramping up the walk, and she thought, *You've waited. Don't spoil it now.* She came slowly to the steps and said in a voice almost shaking, "Be careful of those steps, Frank. I've got all the geraniums on them."

She saw Frank halt and peer down, and then she heard him swear mildly as he tumbled one over in his haste to reach her.

She was in his arms then, and she kissed him lingeringly. For three seconds, she forgot herself, forgot her resolves and her promises to herself, and gave herself to him.

She felt her arm being pulled gently then as he moved her over to the doorway and into the light. She stood there while he leaned against the jamb and looked at her hungrily. Because she was excited and pleased, her small, grave face, her wide green eyes were stirred with pleasure and with love. Her hair, black as a cricket and as shiny, was pinned in careless curls atop her head, and the dress she wore, of some stiff pale yellow stuff, demurely hid the rounded softness of her small body.

Frank only watched her, his face blurred in the half-light, and finally Carrie laughed. "Say something, you fool," she murmured. "All I've heard you say are swear-words."

Frank drew her to him again and kissed her, and then he said, "All right. I'm hungry."

Carrie laughed again, hugged him impulsively, and then went through the doorway into the hall. She hummed a small tune now as she went ahead of him into the big kitchen where the lamp was turned low. She was a fool for being so happy, she knew, but right now it didn't matter. She was grateful enough to live only in the present, right now.

Standing on tiptoe, she turned up the lamp, and then she turned to look at him over her shoulder. He needed a shave, and his short curly hair was tousled, but that could no more blur the edge of him than a stain could blunt the steel of a knife, she thought with a sudden envy. He walked past the counter and in passing reached out and lifted the lid of the cooky crock in the prowling, artless way of a hungry animal, his movements quick and restless. When he caught her watching him his grin came swiftly, touching her heart with fullness, as when she saw a child smile. His friendly, impudent handsomeness would melt stone, she thought, and now he came prowling around the table, and, out of cheerful deviltry, put his arms around her and lifted her off the floor, kissing her neck at the hairline.

"Now put me down," she scolded him. She was aware only then that perhaps there was a sharpness in her voice, and a faint depression touched her and saddened her. It was always this way, when their greeting was over, and the world was as it was instead of made charmed and wonderful by this man she would marry.

She began laying food on the table and Frank dragged one of the chairs out and sat down. He ran his fingers through his short, tousled hair and yawned, and Carrie said, "Bad trip?"

"It was all right going out." He broke off a piece of bread, took a bite of it, and said around it, "How's the Judge?"

"Fine," Carrie said. Her back was to him and now she turned and said over her shoulder, "Before I forget it, he'll want to see you, Frank." He looked up and she said soberly, "About Saber. You own it now."

Frank grimaced and looked at his bread. "I'll have to grow me some mustaches and a belly."

Carrie said lightly, "I'd trade both of them for a couple of roots." As soon as it was out, she regretted saying it. She got out a plate of cold steaks and a dish of cold fried potatoes and set them, along with a pitcher of milk, on the table, and then looked at Frank.

He was watching her, his eyes serious, and said, "All right. I'll grow roots, too."

Carrie poured herself a glass of milk and sat down opposite Frank. He ate silently, swiftly for a moment, and then said, "I'll tell you a story." He raised his fork, and pointed it at her, a frown on his forehead.

Carrie laughed. "Empty your mouth first."

Fork still in the air, Frank chewed a moment on a bite of steak and swallowed it, then waved the fork at her. "I was crossing Roan Creek this morning when I remembered that string of trout pools in Wells Canyon. I cut over to take a look at them—at one pool especially. I've fished it ever since I was a kid, and for one fish." He paused, and lowered his fork. "He's still there."

"The same fish?"

Frank nodded. "The same fish." He looked at his plate, scowling. "That got me to thinking."

"How fat, dumb and happy he was for staying in the same pool?" Carrie asked dryly.

Frank glanced up, a faint shock in his eyes, and Carrie thought swiftly, miserably, *Why do I do that?*

"Yeah," Frank said slowly. "I kind of like him for that, Carrie. I don't think I'll try to catch him any more."

A faint exasperation stirred in Carrie. Fat, dumb and happy had been her own words, but Frank had accepted them, and they described, she thought bitterly, his opinion of men who stayed in the same place for a lifetime. She felt the old skepticism, the old disbelief in him coming back like a wave of nausea, and it frightened her. It laid its dead hand on every hour of her life, and she hated it.

She rose now and went to the counter and cut out a wedge of berry pie, put it on a plate, and returned to the table. Sitting down, she said, "Then you weren't in such a hurry to get back."

"No, I wanted Rob buried," Frank said.

Carrie looked at him pleadingly. "Don't, Frank. He's dead."

"Good," Frank said. He glanced up to see the distaste in Carrie's eyes, and now he shoved the plate of pie away from him. He looked at her levelly and murmured, "I guess we fight tonight."

"Is that new?" Carrie asked bitterly, softly.

Frank reached across the table and took her hand, and his eyes were serious, without humor and without mockery, and Carrie felt a tenseness gather within her. She knew that look in him, and she knew she could not resist it. He said now, "I want to say a lot of things tonight, Carrie. I'm going to, if you won't jump down my throat."

Carrie nodded mutely.

A kind of shadow crawled up into Frank's eyes as he said, "Don't ever expect me to be sorry about Rob dying, or even say I am. There hasn't a dog died in this town in ten years that wasn't mourned more than Rob will be. I know it, and you know it, so let's say it."

Carrie nodded again.

Frank's swift smile came and went, and he was again serious. "But I got Saber from him. I'm going to keep it and I'm going to work it."

He looked at Carrie levelly, waiting, and she didn't move.

"So I think we ought to get married," Frank said.

Carrie regarded him a few bleak seconds, and then withdrew her hand and rose. She said, in as light a voice as she could manage, "Eat your pie, son. You're lightheaded."

She walked over to the counter, and with her back to Frank stood there, her fists clenched, fighting the turmoil inside her. She had waited for this, dreading it, knowing it was coming, and now it was here. She could answer it and end it by simply turning around and saying, "All right," and that was what she had ached to do for five years. But something in her now, as before, told her that it was too easy, and that it would be fatal.

She heard Frank rise, gather up his dishes, take them to the sink and pump water on them. When she turned, her face stiff and expressionless, he was standing by the sink, rolling a cigarette. Without looking at her he said, "You used to laugh when you said no, Carrie. Now you're mad."

"It isn't funny any more, Frank."

Frank dropped his cigarette, pushed away from the sink and came up to her. He put his hand under her chin and tilted it back and waited until she looked at him. "It never was," he said quietly. "I've always meant it."

Carrie reached up and removed his hand and held it between hers. "It's too easy, Frank. I like fairy stories, but I don't believe in them."

"This is one?"

Carrie dipped her head in affirmation.

"The Young Prince who quarrels with the King and leaves? When the King dies, the Young Prince returns to marry the Princess and live happily ever after? Yes, that's one."

"But what if it's so?"

"I want to prove it *with* you," Frank said desperately. "You love me. You can't hide that from me."

"And you love me—when you think of it," Carrie said quietly.

"I'll think of it." He put both hands on her arms and shook

14

her gently. "Carrie, don't look back. We've got Saber. I'll settle down and work it, and we'll have a life nobody's had before. We'll—"

He paused, because Carrie had gently disengaged his hands. She backed off a step now, and said, "You almost make me believe you, Frank—almost." She watched the pain mount in his dark eyes, and knew it was matched in her own, but she went on implacably, "I've waited five years. I'll wait a little longer—until my heart and my head make sense to each other."

There was bitterness in Frank's voice as he said, "And your head says what, Carrie?"

She shook her head. "You wouldn't like to know."

"I want to."

Carrie took a deep breath, because she knew this would hurt, because it was all the truth about him she had learned in these five years. "That you're not only a born drifter, Frank, but that you're a featherweight. That you've never dared try yourself the way a real man must try himself, to find out what he can bear and how he can fight and what he can break. That you run, that you hide or dodge from any trouble that doesn't lie down on its back and roll over when you smile so handsomely." She hesitated. "I—I guess I've said enough."

Frank only nodded, and Carrie was appalled by what she had said. All the life had gone out of his face, all the careless, easy vitality was vanished.

Carrie came to him swiftly then, wrapping her arms around his chest and burying her face in his shirt. "Oh, Frank, don't you see? I've got to know! I'd rather eat my heart out here than have you break it at Saber. I'm not much, but you've got to earn me. You've got to be that fair!"

She felt his hand in her hair and heard him say softly, musingly, "Sure."

There were footsteps on the stairs now, and Carrie knew her father was coming down for his evening walk. She came away from Frank now, and glanced briefly at him, and he gave her his old quick careless smile before he moved around the table and out into the hall. Remembering the smile, Carrie thought bleakly, *It didn't stick. It never will.*

Moving over to the lamp, she blew it out and heard Frank and her father exchange greetings. She went out into the hall in time to hear her father say, "Had something to eat, Frank?"

"I fed him, Dad," Carrie said. "Do you want to talk to him?"

Her father was a spare, gray tall man with a taciturnity in his face that was belied by the mildness of his eyes. He wore a rumpled black suit which was seldom pressed, yet there was an unbending dignity about him that clothes couldn't alter. He had never by word or gesture been anything but courteous to Frank, but now Carrie saw the brief measuring glance he gave Frank and read the distrust there.

"No, my business can wait. It's pretty dull." To Frank he said, "I suppose Carrie told you you're Saber's sole owner now. I'm Rob's executor, and we'll have papers to sign."

Frank nodded, and asked idly, "Who saw Rob afterwards, Judge?"

Judge Tavister looked at him sharply. "I didn't hear. The usual people, I suppose—coroner, sheriff, and jury." When Frank said nothing, her father looked at her. "Well, I'm going for my walk. Good night, Frank."

"Be careful of those flowerpots," Carrie said.

"I know. I've been hurdling the damned things for years."

Carrie smiled and looked at Frank, but he was watching the Judge's disappearing back with a sober thoughtfulness. When her father was out of sight, Carrie said, "Why did you ask him about Rob?"

Frank shrugged, and when he looked at her the old impudence and mockery and fun was back in his face. "Practicing," he murmured. "I'll have to talk to my father-in-law about something." He came over and kissed her and said, "I'll be back from Saber as soon as I can."

She went to the door with him and watched him pick his way through the geraniums, and then she leaned against the doorjamb until he had mounted and ridden out. Afterwards she sorted out the promises he had made her tonight, weighing them against other promises he had made in the past. Presently, she said aloud to the night and to herself, in a discouraged voice, "Maybe," and went inside.

Chapter 3

At the corner, Frank turned in the saddle and saw Carrie's small figure outlined against the light in the hall. When he faced ahead again, he shook his head once in dislike of the gray and troubling thoughts within him. There was no way to explain to her that the words he had used once did not have the same meaning now, that a promise given and broken ten times could be kept the eleventh. No, he had used that coin with her until it had no value, and he must start over, now, and he accepted this tranquilly in the quiet night.

In the middle of the next block, he saw the dim figure of Judge Tavister halted on the sidewalk in the deep shade of the roadside trees. The Judge came out to the road and called quietly, "Frank," and Frank kneed his sorrel over to the edge of the street.

Judge Tavister was carrying his hat; in the almost unbroken darkness, Frank could not see the expression on his face.

"Why did you ask that question about Rob?" Judge Tavister asked him.

"Somebody said Hannan isn't sure Rob's death was an accident."

"What else did somebody say?"

Frank hesitated, reluctant to say this. "That Hannan might suspect me of his murder."

There was a long silence, and then Judge Tavister said, "Frank, what did you and Rob have that last quarrel about?"

"My general uselessness," Frank said tonelessly. "He wanted me to work under Jess until I knew Saber's business. I already knew it, and I wouldn't stay around him." He paused, groping for words, and then said wanly, "One thing led to another."

"Fists?"

"No," Frank said quickly. "He hit me, and I let him." He was remembering now. "He said he was sorry he'd ever gone near the wagon train and found me. Said he was sorry the Utes didn't get me along with my folks. He said they must have known I'd do more damage to the whites than fifty Indians, and that's why they let me live. He said—" He hesitated.

"Yes?" Judge Tavister prompted mildly.

Frank shifted in the saddle and said in a dull matter-of-fact voice: "He said before he buried my mother he looked for a wedding ring and couldn't find it. She wore other rings, but no wedding ring. He said she looked as if she came out of a House —a cheap House."

"Ah," Judge Tavister said, a faint disgust in his voice. "Does Hannan have to know he said that?"

"He knows it," Frank said shortly. "Rob said it in the bunkhouse in front of the whole crew. I left then."

There was an unrunning silence, and then Judge Tavister said gently, "Why didn't you stay away, Frank?"

"Carrie," Frank answered promptly.

"That's the reason you should have," Judge Tavister said softly.

"That's the way you've felt all along, isn't it, Judge?"

"No man likes to see his child unhappy," the Judge said quietly. "He'll change it if he can."

"You can't."

"You'll have a lot of offers for Saber," Judge Tavister went on. "That always happens when a man dies. Take the best offer and get out. This is a big country—as I think you've proved to yourself."

"And run away once more," Frank murmured.

"Yes. From what you're bound to hurt."

Frank tried to see Judge Tavister's face in the darkness and could not. He said slowly, "If I hurt her again, I'll go."

"What if you can't help but hurt her again?"

Frank scowled, turning this over in his mind, making many things of it. "Speak plainer, Judge."

"All right, what if Hannan decides rightly or wrongly that you murdered Rob. It could happen. You've got a reputation around here for being good-natured, good-looking and good-for-nothing, Frank, and people will envy you getting Saber. What if you wait it out in jail for a trial? The verdict doesn't matter. What about Carrie then?"

There was, Frank saw, a bitter truth in all this, and yet there was something else too that the Judge didn't see. "If I sell Saber and drift, that's admitting I'm afraid of what Hannan will turn up. It's admitting I'm not worth much."

"I'm not interested in it."

"Even if I'm innocent?"

Judge Tavister was silent a long, long moment, as if he were searching his mind for the most honest of answers. "No," he said then, a strange implacability in his voice, "Not even then. Because you really aren't worth anything, Frank—not even an hour's unhappiness for Carrie."

Frank said gently, "More than that, Judge," and put his horse in motion and moved on down the quiet street. *I've gone a long way down the road if he thinks that,* he reflected bitterly. And this judgment, too, like Carrie's, would have to wait on time, until the old label had worn off, he knew.

He turned at the corner now, heading for the main four-corners. The cool mountain evening was all around him, smelling of resin and the river, full of the low rush of the distant river, too. He paused at the four-corners, looking across at the Pleasant Hour Saloon in the middle of the block. Chances were that Hannan, if he were still in town, would be there, and Frank understood now that his business with the sheriff was urgent. He angled across the street to the Pleasant Hour's tie-rail, and before dismounting he looked over the line of ponies racked there. Several of them bore Rhino Hulst's J-1 brand, and one of them was Hugh Nunnally's. The crew was back, and with them, he knew, lay the power to still Hannan's curiosity.

Shouldering his way through the swing doors, he tramped over to the long bar on his right, looking over the big, brightly lit room. Several rear tables were occupied by poker players. A monte game just beyond the bar had drawn a small crowd, and in that crowd Frank saw the big stoop-shouldered frame of Buck Hannan. Beyond, at one of the poker tables, he saw Rhino's bunch—Pete Faraday, Albie Beecham, Morg Lister, and Bill Talley, with Hugh Nunnally, whose broad back was to the door.

The two McGarrity brothers were at the bar, and Frank halted beside Jonas, the younger brother. Jonas was a tall, workworn man in the rough clothes of a ranch hand; John, the older brother, wore a neat black suit, and his mild, cheerful face made him look years younger than his brother. Together, they operated a growing freighting company, and themselves worked at jobs which ranged from teamstering to bookkeeping, with a stubborn skill.

Jonas had seen Frank in the mirror of the back bar, and his morose face broke in the start of a smile. "I been needin' you, Frank," he said, turning now. "We can use some new teams."

"See Rhino," Frank said. He asked the bartender for whiskey.

John McGarrity leaned back and said around Jonas, "Hell with Rhino. The last horse we bought from him died of sand colic in a week."

Frank shook his head and smiled to take the edge off his refusal. "I've quit, gents. You're on your own." He took his whiskey and moved back through the room, hearing Jonas swear in mild frustration. As he had anticipated, Buck Hannan broke away from the monte game watchers and intercepted him. "In a hurry, Frank?"

Frank halted. Buck Hannan was a big, soft, smooth-faced man of fifty, pleasant with the meaningless affability of an elected public servant, but his sharp gray eyes were alert and searching. He was coatless, his black trousers tucked into burnished half-boots, and he wore no badge of office on his checked shirt.

He shook hands and looked about him and spotted an empty gaming table. Still holding Frank's hand, he said, "Let's sit down. Thought you might want to know about Rob."

Frank said he did, and they took chairs. Frank saw Rhino's bunch watching him; Pete Faraday, Rhino's half-breed Ute wagon-master, leaned across his cards and murmured something to Hugh Nunnally, whose square and blocky face turned toward Frank.

Hannan offered Frank a cigar, which he refused, lighted one himself, and then said in a respectful voice, "I know how you feel about this, Frank. I know—"

"How do I?" Frank cut in.

Buck Hannan's gaze altered into hardness. "All right, how do you?"

"I'm glad he's dead, Buck," Frank said bluntly. "You can make anything out of that you want."

"Now, what would I make out of it?" Buck asked mildly.

"Lots of things. That I murdered him, so I hear."

"People talk too much," Hannan said, still mildly. He had never ceased watching Frank, noting each change of expression, weighing what he noted.

"How did he die?" Frank asked.

"Why, his back was broken, and somebody stuck a knife between his ribs a couple of times."

Frank made no comment; his face was contained, non-committal, and Buck Hannan shook his head. "So you're glad?" he observed.

Frank said thinly: "What do you want to know, Buck? That we fought all the time? That I was broke? That Saber is a big outfit?"

Hannan shook his head slowly. "No, I know all that. What I want to know is where you've been the last month."

Frank noticed his drink now. He drank it, said, "Come along," rose, and led the way over to the table where Hulst's crew was seated.

Hugh Nunnally looked up as Frank halted beside him. He was a short, blocky man, under thirty, with a sleepy indolence about his every movement. He was Rhino's first man, a born horse-trader with an astute knowledge of horses, a nerveless gall, and a devious mind, all smothered skillfully by a slow smile and the steady guileless eyes of a simple and satisfied man. Of the thirty men Rhino worked on and off his horse lot, Nunnally was absolute boss. He shared in all of Rhino's countless deals, and he was the key figure in them all, from the sly sucker's game from which he and Frank had just returned to the hiring and paying of the secret and furtive men who passed into Rhino's office, talked behind closed doors, and disappeared. He wore a stained calico shirt, and his last shave had been days ago, so that his beard stubble, the same pale color as his thick hair under its tattered hat, gave him the air of an amiable and unwashed line rider.

He nodded and grinned at Hannan, and Frank said, "Hugh, Hannan wants to know where I've been the last month."

Hugh frowned, regarding Frank lazily, and then he shifted his glance to Hannan. "Every place, Buck. Hell, when you buy horses, you cover a lot of ground."

"Not you," Hannan said. "Chess here. He been traveling with someone all the time?"

Hugh glanced again at Frank, and there was an odd and mild malice in his pale eyes. "Were you, Frank?"

Frank felt a cold premonition stirring within him now. Rhino and Hugh, just as much as himself, had to hide the facts of the Army-officer swindle. The only way that could be done was for Nunnally to give immediate proof that Frank was never alone in the three months they'd been gone, so Hannan wouldn't pry. Yet Nunnally was hesitating.

A kind of wary panic was in Frank then. If he was on his own, he must be cautious, and he answered slowly, "Not always with someone, Hugh."

Nunnally looked up at Hannan now. "We were all over that country, Buck—singly and in pairs and the whole bunch. We'd hear of a Mormon with a good bunch of horses. One of us would go to his place to look 'em over. If it was a big bunch and they looked good, we'd buy and send for help to drive them back to the herd." He frowned. "What's all this about, anyhow?"

"Was Chess alone long enough for him to ride back here without the rest of you knowing it?" Hannan persisted.

Here it is, Frank thought. Nunnally's glance, faintly mocking, lifted to Frank's face, and Frank tried to still his excitement.

Hugh scratched his head and said in a thoughtful voice, "Why, I don't know, Buck. He might have been. I never kept track of him much. He knows a good horse, and what Rhino'd pay for one. He'd get money from me and bring in the horses. I knew about where he was going, and that's all." He repeated then, more demandingly, "What's this all about, anyway, We just got in town."

Frank saw the chagrin mount in Hannan's eyes. "In other words," Hannan said grimly, "you didn't pay any attention. You didn't know where he was."

"Why should I?" Nunnally demanded innocently.

Hannan didn't answer him; he looked speculatively at Frank and said grimly, "Ask Frank," and turned on his heel and walked off.

Now the anger came, and there was a wicked rage in Frank's eyes as he looked at Hugh.

"Tell us, Frank," Nunnally said slyly.

Frank said thinly, "Let's go where we can talk, Hugh."

Nunnally laughed soundlessly. "I've got something to say to you, but let's wait till you cool off."

"You'll come or I'll drag you out," Frank said with an ominous quietness.

Nunnally's eyes changed faintly, hardening, narrowing. "You couldn't drag me out of a deep sleep," he said flatly. He looked searchingly at Frank for a moment. "Maybe I will, at that."

Pete Faraday, the Ute half-breed, started to rise. Frank put a hand on his shoulder and pushed him down in his chair. "You stay out of this," he said. He looked at the others now, and said, "You, too," and turned and tramped toward the rear of the room. Passing the two small cubbyholes which were private card rooms, he stepped out the back door onto the loading platform that ran across the rear of the building and which was stacked with empty beer barrels at its far end.

He moved away from the door and halted, and Nunnally came up and halted too. His hands were on his hips, and every line of his blocky form was arrogant and pugnacious.

A hard recklessness was in Frank now that he didn't try to check. "You could have pulled Hannan off my neck in there, Hugh. Why didn't you?"

"We want you back in your soldier suit," Nunnally said slowly. "We'll lose money without you."

"I told Rhino I'd quit."

"Maybe you'll change your mind, now." Nunnally laughed quietly. "You're licked, Chess. Hannan hasn't dropped this because I left it open—purposely. He'll be at me and the boys again and again. You come back to Rhino and I'll account to Hannan for every day you were gone. Get stubborn about it, and we can start remembering the days nobody saw you." He paused. "Or you can tell him what you were really doing."

"Who was I working for?"

"And who wore the uniform?" Hugh asked dryly.

A gray hopelessness touched Frank then. In breaking with Rhino and his whole shabby crew, he had counted on Rhino's silence about the uniform, because if it became known they would both be in trouble. But Rhino had sidestepped that problem, working his blackmail in a more subtle way. Rob's death

23

and Hannan's suspicion had given him the opening, and Hugh had summed up the result. The alternative was to tell Hannan the truth, and when that became known he would lose Carrie as surely as if he had died. *If I lost her, I wouldn't want to live,* he thought. But a black and savage stubbornness would not let him return to Rhino. He had turned that corner, never to go back.

He was silent so long Nunnally said dryly, "Figured it out?"

"I've figured it," Frank said grimly. "I told Rhino I've quit. I have."

"I hate a fool," Nunnally said contemptuously. "Listen to me. Do you want to be tried by Tavister and hung in front of Carrie?"

"For killing you," Frank said softly.

It took Nunnally several seconds to read into those three words what Frank had intended should be read. Then Hugh slapped him with his open palm, and said, "You aren't tough, friend. You never were."

On the heels of his last word, Frank lashed out at him. The blow caught Nunnally in the face, and it surprised him. He stood motionless a moment, and then he lunged.

The impact of their meeting shook the platform, and one of the beer barrels toppled over. Hugh wrapped his huge arms around Frank, and Frank, slugging viciously at Hugh's midriff, stamped on Hugh's feet.

The punishment forced Nunnally to break away, and Frank took a step backward. Suddenly, his arms were grabbed from behind and pinned in an iron grip. He wrestled savagely, smelling the rank Indian smell of Pete Faraday against him, and he cursed himself for not having remembered Pete's blind loyalty to Nunnally.

After a moment, he saw struggle was useless; Pete's knee was in his back, keeping him off balance, putting him on the tips of his toes that could not hold his weight.

He subsided finally, shaking with rage, and he saw Nunnally approach and plant his feet apart, getting his stance to hit him.

Nunnally hesitated then, and finally said, "Let him go, Pete."

Pete let go his arms. Frank, wheeling now, half-turned and looped a smashing right that caught the half-breed flush in the throat.

Faraday had been standing close to the edge of the platform. He fell backwards now, clawing at the air, and landed solidly on his back in the cinders four feet below.

A wild rage was in Frank now. He leaped off the platform, landing astride the half-breed, and he pumped blow after blow into Faraday's face.

Nunnally acted quickly; he vaulted to the cinders, pulling his gun with his right hand. Raising it level with his right shoulder, he brought the barrel down smartly against Frank's head.

Frank pitched forward across Faraday's face, and Nunnally, leaning down, dragged him free of the half-breed. Faraday came unsteadily to his feet then, his hand to his nose which was streaming blood.

Nunnally pulled a handkerchief from his pocket and extended it, saying, "Here, you damn fool."

Pete accepted it and then turned slowly to look at Frank, who was sprawled motionless on his face in the cinders.

"He drunk?" Faraday asked wonderingly.

"Stone-sober," Nunnally said slowly. He too was looking at Frank, his mild eyes speculative and indrawn. "He's feeling pious now. That'll last about a week."

Chapter 4

BEYOND THE UPPER end of town, Frank took the wagon road branching left where the long lift to the Battle Meadows and Saber began. His head ached throbbingly, and the drink he had bought at the Pleasant Hour before leaving town sat cold and unwanted within him.

Around midnight, he forded lower Elk Creek and let his horse drink, afterward following the creek for another half-hour through vaulting pine timber until he came to the first small meadow of Saber's range. It had rained here today; he could smell the black moist earth under the standing wild hay, and the breeze was almost chill. Crossing the meadows that drained the shouldering pine-clad Battle Peaks to the east, he heard cattle moving away from him in the night.

Presently, at the far end of the meadows he made out the dark scattering of Saber's buildings abutting the black pines. The place was dark, sleeping, and he was thankful for that.

A dog picked him up before he reached the outbuildings, and Frank cursed him into silence. At the corral beside the big barn he unsaddled, turned his horse into the pasture, and tramped toward the house. The log bunkhouse and cookshack lay between the outbuildings and the house, and as he approached it he saw a figure standing in the dark doorway. It called, "Who's that?" and Frank said, "Me, Jess, Frank."

"Oh." There was a faint undertone of resignation and of disappointment that Frank did not miss before Jess Irby said, "Wait'll I get a light, Frank."

"Go back to sleep," Frank said. "I'll see you in the morning."

Jess grunted assent, and Frank tramped on, heading for the right wing of the big two-story log house that loomed before him now. His homecoming, he knew, would bring a welcome from nobody. Long since, Jess Irby and the Saber crew had written him off as trifling, and as a drifter whose occasional returns to Saber always meant trouble.

Just inside the yard fence a big pine lifted high into the night sky, one of its lower branches scraping noisily on the weathered shingles of the house at each stirring of the wind.

Frank let himself into the unlocked office, struck a match, and lighted the lamp atop the roll-top desk pushed against the back wall. He looked around him now; nothing was changed, from the big spreading long-horns mounted on a musty green velvet that hung over the desk to the comfortable litter of magazines, bridles, odd bits of leather, guns, traps, and utility clothes that lay scattered about the broken leather sofa, the deep chair and the unswept floor. This was Jess Irby's domain, the ranch office, the part of the house he liked.

He picked up the lamp and opened the door in the rear wall that led onto the hall. Turning left here, he was in the living room.

Holding the lamp overhead now, he looked about him, and the sight of its gilt trashiness brought a flood of ancient and unwelcome memories to him. Here were the tastes of a dozen of Rob Custis' women recorded in tarnished gilt mirrors, in fluffy pillows, in ornate lamps. He moved slowly across the room to the hall opposite, tag ends of dim memory made vivid by the room. Who were the women, and where had they gone? Some of their names and faces were part of his childhood; some were pretty, some drunken, some cruel, all indifferent to the growing waif Rob had tolerated around the house.

He remembered the weeks of carousing, the nights made hideous and wakeful by singing and shouting and fighting. Those were the times he ate at the cookshack and rode with the crew, and often when he came back the house was empty and Rob was gone. There were months on end when he never saw school, when he ran in the brush with the half-wild Ute kids, and nobody knew where he was, or cared. There were times, too, when Rob returned, sometimes with a new woman, sometimes alone, but there were always beatings and threats and a harshly policed life. Sometimes there were presents, too, so many and so lavish as to numb him; other times, there were only Rob's bitter black silences, his indifference and his savage discipline. The only thing that had stayed constant through the years was Saber itself, its vaulting mountain ranges and its cattle, kept so only by Rob's hard-headed greed.

He went on into the opposite hall that led him past two closed doors, and he turned into the end room. This was his room; it had been his since the first day he came.

Moving across it, he put the lamp on the table, then opened the outside door, letting the fresh night air drive out the musty smell of disuse. A bare iron bed and a single chair beside the washstand comprised the furniture. He pulled off his boots, and then peeled out of his shirt, and as he threw his boots across the room he saw the bullet hole in the wall. He regarded it thoughtfully, remembering the day long ago when he had stolen Rob's new Sharp's rifle, hiding it under his covers until nighttime, when he could try it. In the darkness he had fondled it, admiring it, and finally he had sighted it at the wall. He hadn't meant to fire it, but somehow that happened, and Rob had raged, baffled at the wildness of this orphan he had never tried to break until it was too late.

He rolled a pair of cigarettes now, placed them beside him

27

on the washstand, lighted one, and stretched out on the bed. *I wish he'd broken me*, he thought now with an unaccustomed bitterness.

For he saw with new clarity the cause of his trouble, and the end of it. He had accepted the wearing of Rhino's stolen uniform out of some wild and reckless protest against the words Rob had spoken that night in the bunkhouse. In a way he could not explain, those words were the cruelest he would ever listen to. All the self-doubt that he had known in his life with Rob had been confirmed by those words—he was the unwanted son of a cheap woman and an anonymous father. It had taken him three weary months to accept that, to reason away the shame and the hopelessness, but those three months had done the harm. For he knew that Carrie would accept his irresponsibility with a patient hope that he would change, but she would never accept his crookedness. He would stand trial for Rob's murder before he would let that come out. And then, sickeningly, he knew he would do neither. This house, these cattle and these acres were his, and he was rich, and he would give them all to wipe out these three months past.

And then a thought came to him, and its strangeness brought him slowly to a sitting position on the bed. *Why do I have to accept Saber?* he thought; *if I don't take it till Rob's murderer is found, Hannan can't say I killed him for it.* He lay back now, his mind roiled with excitement. Would that pull Hannan off him? It would, because once this motive for his killing Rob was removed, there was only the motive of hatred left. And Frank knew grimly that his hatred for Rob was shared by a half a hundred people here that Rob had bullied and swindled and trampled over.

As for losing Saber, he didn't care. He had fifty or sixty horses up in the hills, the only things he could call his own. He'd start from scratch, and show Carrie he was in dead earnest.

When, minutes later, he blew the lamp, he felt a deep peace.

The clanging of the triangle, the cook's call to breakfast, awakened him next morning. He dressed hurriedly and went out, and by the time he reached the cookshack, the last hand had gone in. He washed at the bench which stood just outside the bunkhouse door, and combed his hair.

As he turned toward the cookshack door, a subtle change came into his face, altering it with a faint grimness. The men inside were the same men who had witnessed his exit three months ago. They had heard Rob name him, and had seen Rob hit him, and while they had remained aloof and silent that evening, he knew they thought Rob half right. A handful of them, the old hands like Jess Irby, had even taught him to judge a horse and fatten a steer and keep simple books, grooming him for the job he had contemptuously thrown in Rob's face that last night.

A comfortable clamor of tinware filled the big room as he entered. The fifteen men of Saber's crew lined each side of a long table in the center of the room. At his entrance, the men looked up, and Jess Irby rose from his place at the end of the table.

Saber's foreman was a tall man in his sixties, slow-moving, with a white down-slanting mustache in a sun-blackened, seamed face, and the big hand he held out to Frank was dry and leathery. His eyes, a frosty blue, were reserved, neutral, as he said, "Thought you were about due, son. Take a plate."

There was a vacant place halfway down the table, and Frank, heading for it, touched a tall, balding puncher on the shoulder and said, "Hello, Red." His greeting was returned. From some of the others, he received reserved nods, and still others carefully stared at their plates. There were three or four new faces; all the rest were old Saber hands, proud, competent—and hostile.

Frank stepped over the bench into the vacant place between Joe Rich and old Cass Hardesty, the blacksmith. Across from him sat Johnny Samuels, the youngest hand in the crew. Johnny's single year at Saber had taken the edge off his cockiness and steadied him, for it was Jess Irby's way to load a new man with enough responsibility to make him or break him. Johnny passed over a tin plate of hot cakes to Frank, and their glances met. The reserve Johnny had cultivated was not yet deep enough to hide the dislike in his eyes, and Frank saw it and met it with a quiet indifference.

Old Cass Hardesty from beside him asked pleasantly, "Make any money for yourself, Frank?"

29

"For Rhino, mostly," Frank answered.

Johnny Samuels observed quietly, "That's one thing you can quit worrying about now, Frank."

Frank said easily, "I never did worry much about it, Johnny."

"That's right. You never worried about it," Johnny agreed soberly.

Frank was aware that the whole table, while eating, was listening. He was further aware that they were understandably uneasy about the change of ownership, for while Rob had been a savage tyrant, he had not been a fool, and he had let his crew alone. Frank checked a quick answer and set about eating.

Presently, Johnny said, "When do you figure to sell, Frank?"

Swift anger touched Frank then. "I figured Jess was foreman here, Johnny."

"He is. Foreman for who, though? The bank? A company?" There was a deep and mounting resentment in Johnny's voice then as he added, "Or any stranger that trimmed you in a poker game?"

"Johnny!" Jess said sharply.

Frank put down his fork. "You talk too much," he said quietly.

Johnny Samuels put down his fork too. "I can do something else besides talk, though. I've never seen you do much else."

There was a limit, Frank knew, to what he must pay for the past, and this went beyond it. He rose, reached across the table and grabbed Johnny Samuels' blond hair in a hard grip, and with his right hand he hit Johnny along his shelving jaw. He hit him once, and let go his hair, and said thinly, "You've seen me do that."

Johnny came boiling out of his seat. He mounted the bench, stepped on the table, and dived across it at Frank.

As if this were a prearranged signal, the whole room exploded into action. Jim Desert and fat Roy Shields, who had been sitting on either side of Johnny, came onto and across the table at the same time. Joe Rich slugged Frank in the belly; Cass Hardesty leaped on his back and wrapped a sinewy arm under his chin. Frank staggered back against the wall now, Cass still on his back. Bracing himself, he put his head down and fought blindly, savagely, and the crew fought among themselves to get at him, to hit him, to kick him. He knew with a gray despair that this was their revenge for his undeserved luck, for the years he had idled while they worked.

The rain of blows on his chest, belly, and face drove the breath from him, and the pain of them was a numbing thing that weighted his arms with lead. He fought stubbornly, ferociously, a feral anger twisting his face.

And then a shotgun boomed in the room, filling it with a deafening roar, and Jess Irby's voice followed on the heel of it. "Get away from him or I'll shoot you in the back!"

Cass dropped off Frank's back, and the others backed off. Frank leaned against the wall, hands at his sides, head hung, dragging in great gusts of breath, and now he heard rather than saw Jess Irby roughly shoving his way through the crew.

Jess said roughly, "Have the whole bunch of you gone crazy!"

Old Cass Hardesty muttered, "Hell, you don't have to be crazy to want to hit him. I been wanting to for six years."

Johnny Samuels said, "Yeah. I'm glad you got it before you fired us, Frank."

Frank took a deep breath, wiping the blood from his nose with his sleeve. His shirt was half-torn off, his chest livid with bruises, and it hurt to breathe. Looking over the crew he saw the residue of anger in their faces, and of a wicked pleasure, too.

He said: "I'm not giving anyone his time unless he wants it. Jess is running this outfit and he'll keep running it. I got Saber by accident. I'm not taking a penny from it until Rob's killer is found, and I'm not running it."

He paused, and nobody said anything. Pushing away from the wall he said: "I'm going to be trading horses, and I'll live in my room and work out from Saber. I'll be around here a lot." He looked at each man directly now. "I'll take exactly as much ridin' from you as I'd take from any man." He looked now at Johnny. "You know how much that is, Johnny?"

Johnny didn't answer.

"None," Frank said flatly. He moved past Jess and went out the door, leaving the room silent.

Chapter 5

T ESS FALETTE was making out a waybill for a waiting teamster when old Mr. Shinner paused by her desk in the late
afternoon and said in his dry and worried voice, "Mr. Hulst
would like to see you."

"All right," Tess said. She went on writing, and Shinner,
after waiting a moment, said, "Right now."

"Go away," Tess said. Shinner sniffed and went over to his
desk. Tess finished the waybill and handed it to the teamster,
a big, sulky-looking man. She said in a matter-of-fact voice,
"If you hadn't come in drunk this morning, Bill, you'd be
ten hours on the way now."

The teamster said morosely, "This ain't no time to start.
It's quittin' time, almost."

"But you'll start," Tess said firmly.

The teamster rammed the waybill in his pocket, and then
grinned slowly. "I only had a drop, Miss Falette. Nothin'
wrong with that, is there?"

"Not if it isn't the drop too much," Tess said. "It always is
with you. Now, get along."

The teamster tramped out and Tess looked over her desk.
Things were pretty well cleaned up for the day, and she
stretched luxuriously. She was aware that Shinner was watching her disapprovingly and almost fearfully, for the boss had
spoken and she had not jumped. He was a little gray man
with a little gray mind, and out of some perverse wish to tease
him, Tess rose, went through the gate in the railing, but
instead of turning down the corridor, she strolled to the outside door. She paused here, looking over the lot, and watched
Bill Schulte climb into the high-sided freight wagon and whip
his six horses into movement. As he passed the office, he saw
her standing in the doorway and he called out, "Good-bye,
honey-sweetheart," and guffawed loudly.

32

Tess regarded him coldly, not moving, and presently she turned and went down the corridor and stepped into Rhino's office.

Rhino was standing at the open window; he was so tall he had to stoop to see out. Now he turned and looked at her and nodded toward the lot. "That happen often?"

"Often enough, but I can handle it," Tess said.

"There'll be no more of that," Rhino observed grimly. "Sit down, please."

Tess settled into the chair pulled up beside his desk, and folded her hands on the lap of her drab office dress. She noted without interest that the sleeves of her dress were getting shiny and that her fingers were ink-stained.

Rhino sat down heavily in his oversize swivel chair and laid a massive hand on top of some papers on his desk. "I've finished these," he said pleasantly, and he frowned a little. "Are you sure your figures are right?"

Tess smiled a little. "The money's in the bank, Mr. Hulst."

"I can't believe it," Rhino said slowly. "Frankly, when I gave over the freighting end to you, I'd have been satisfied if you'd paid your salary out of it. The thing was a nuisance."

"A money-making nuisance."

"How've you done it?" Rhino asked in his kindly voice. "What's happened to the McGarrity boys? You've taken a nick out of their business, haven't you?"

"No, we can each do one thing best, and we do it," Tess replied. "We can haul freight downriver at a rate they can't touch, and they won't even try. But from Leadville over to here, we can't buck them. We each go our own way."

Rhino's eyes sharpened. "Why can we beat them downriver, but not upriver?"

"We're hauling feed for the lot in from downriver all the time," Tess said. "The wagons used to go down empty. Now I load them with freight, so we're full coming and going, and can offer a lower rate. The McGarritys' wagons have to come back empty, and it doesn't pay them."

Rhino smiled and nodded appreciatively. "What about upriver?"

Tess shook her head. "The McGarritys have us there.

33

They've got good wagons and good teamsters, and they keep a schedule."

"And we haven't?"

Tess laughed. "Bill's a sample of the teamsters Hugh gives me. Anybody half drunk or sick or who can't do a day's work is a teamster. For wagons we use anything lying around the lot. For teams we've been using half-wild range horses that we want broken for harness." She shrugged now. "As for a schedule, we couldn't keep one at the point of a gun."

Rhino put back his head and laughed, and Tess smiled too. She had never complained of her tools before, and now that the opportunity had come she wondered if it would do any good. She was a woman in a man's world, she knew, yet Rhino seemed interested enough.

He said now, "What do you need?"

"Sound freight wagons," Tess said promptly. "Real working teamsters, not saloon bums. Good teams broken to harness."

"Think you could run the McGarritys up a tree, then?"

"I wouldn't try."

Rhino frowned, puzzled, and Tess leaned forward a little. "Look, Mr. Hulst. Plenty of freight outfits in Denver City and Leadville book freight on through to points in Utah and even Salt Lake, don't they?"

Rhino nodded.

"Well, the McGarritys have an agent in Leadville. Let him book freight on through to Utah too. The McGarritys can haul it this far and transfer to our wagons. We can haul it to the Utah points and still bring back all our feed. With our low rates tacked onto the McGarritys' rates, we could haul cheaper than other outfits and both of us would make more money than we do now."

Rhino scowled and half-swung his chair around to look out the window. His big hands lay on his massive thighs, and a thick third finger tapped regularly on his frayed trousers. Tess wondered again at the worn clothes Rhino affected, and guessed shrewdly that a horse-trader, which Rhino had once been, could never afford to seem too prosperous. Rhino scrubbed his chin thoughtfully and turned to regard her. "A sound idea," he murmured, "but why make money for the Mc-Garritys? Why don't we do it all?"

"They've got the good equipment. We can't buck them without spending a lot of money."

Rhino pursed his lips doubtfully. "What would happen if we hauled freight from Leadville to points in Utah for ninety cents a hundred?"

"You'd lose money."

"But I'd get the business. What else would happen, though? Would the McGarrity boys match that rate?"

"They couldn't, and stay in business," Tess said.

"Exactly," Rhino murmured. He laced his fingers behind his head and stared benevolently at the ceiling. "I've made some money this summer I'd like to gamble with," he said, and now he looked sharply at her. "Do you think the McGarritys have money behind them—or could get it?"

Tess frowned. "No. They've got where they are by hard work and little money."

Rhino smiled. "What would happen then if I threw away a few thousand dollars by cutting rates until they couldn't meet them?"

"You'd ruin them," Tess said quietly.

Rhino detected the censure in her words, and he raised his eyebrows. "And if I do?"

"I like them," Tess said simply. "They're good men."

Rhino chuckled. "It's your privilege to like them—after working hours."

Tess was silent, appalled by what was shaping up. She said now in a quick and curious voice, "You mean you'd break them to make money, Mr. Hulst?"

Rhino smiled, and nodded. "I'll throw away up to ten thousand cutting rates. By that time, they'll be out of business and we can pick up their wagons cheap, maybe the whole outfit. After that, I can hoist rates and make back my ten thousand."

Tess sat utterly motionless now. She was remembering Jonas McGarrity, that big, loose-framed, gangling man who had spent a score of nights telling her of his deep ambitions, watching her to see if he stirred affection or love in her, and finally being content with her friendship. He was a good man, simple and kind and tolerant, and all his homely hopes along with his brother's were doomed now by Rhino's greed. It was the heartlessness of Rhino's plan that frightened her. If a man with a few thousand dollars in the bank could drive two other men to ruin, something was wrong. It was as if she had glimpsed something black and slimy and nameless that she was not meant to look upon, and she turned away from it instinctively.

"Well?" Rhino said. "What's wrong with that idea?"

"What do I do about it?" Tess asked reluctantly. She would not look at him; she kept pleating the folds of her drab skirt.

"Go see the McGarritys. Tell them what we're going to do. Unless they're fools, they'll see they're licked. Get their offer on the whole outfit and bring it to me, and we'll see how it looks."

Tess stood up, looking at a point beyond Rhino's head. "Isn't that a job for a man?" she asked woodenly.

Rhino shook his head. "You, my dear, are running the freighting end. I supply only the money and advice."

Tess said good night and went back to her desk. Shinner had shoved his books in the safe, and now he bade her a precise good evening as he went out. Tess sat down slowly at her desk and stared at the dingy wall opposite. There was a price on everything, she thought bitterly, and this was the price on her job, that she must ruin the McGarritys. She remembered now that the McGarritys yesterday had come in to rent four teams for a special hauling job of mine machinery to Meeker, the mining camp back in the mountains. They would be home tomorrow, and tomorrow night, she knew, she would have to face them.

She heard someone mounting the steps and turned to see Hugh Nunnally tramp in, heading for Rhino's office. He grinned lazily and said, "You've had enough for today, Tess. Go home."

"On my way," Tess said.

Hugh went on through to the office and Tess stared at the corridor doorway. It seemed to her now that it wasn't just a plain doorway in a shabby, ill-lit office any more but an entrance to a dark cave where a cunning old man wove his secret schemes and laughed at pity.

She rose now and swiftly cleared her desk, and she could

barely control the impulse to get out of here and as far away as her legs would take her. She had just twenty-four hours to get used to the idea of being a partner in a crime. *I'll think of a way around it,* she thought then, and she wondered desperately if she could.

Chapter 6

THE HOLDING CORRAL Frank elected to work out from lay on the upper Elk among the aspens, Saber's highest range. Here, the Elk broke out of a steep-walled canyon into a flat hay meadow, and a high fence of peeling aspen poles stretched across the canyon's mouth.

Two hours before dusk the dozen horses inside the corral lifted their ears alertly and looked out toward the meadow. Twenty-odd horses broke out of the aspens now into the meadow, loping for the creek.

Frank reined in at the edge of the timber, letting the band he had been driving seek water. Looking over the near peaks to the east, he saw a long flat slate-covered cloud drifting mares' tails of rain onto the boulder fields to the north. If rain came, it would be after dark, and he had a good hour of working light.

His camp lay under three stunted pines along the stream; passing it now he saw the tarp covering his gear pooled with water from the rain that had soaked him that afternoon.

At the corral, he herded the dozen horses already inside back into the canyon, and stretched a pair of ropes from one side of the canyon across to the other to hold them there.

Leaving the corral gate open now, he mounted and swung in a wide half-circle around the twenty new horses he had been driving, and came up behind them. They moved docilely into the corral and Frank closed the gate.

On this, his second evening out of Saber, he still moved with a stiff weariness as he off-saddled and turned his horse loose to graze. Back in camp, he built up a fire, filled a coffeepot from the creek and set it to boil. Afterward, he rummaged around and found a cold biscuit to chew on, then took up his rope and headed back for the corral. His step was slow; a grinding weariness was on him, and the day's riding which had begun before sunup had been a minor torture. His ribs were so sore that even breathing was an effort, and every movement this day had reminded him of the welcome he had received at the hands of Saber's crew.

Inside the corral, he stubbornly set about the wearisome job of cutting out his own horses from the general bunch and pushing them back into the rope corral with the others. It had taken him two days of hard work to round up and cut out a third of his own string—a job that, with another man, would have been a bare day's job.

At deep dusk, he was finished. He turned out the unwanted horses, and looked briefly at the eighteen he had kept. Even now, he had no certain idea why he was doing this, except that these horses represented his fortune and his future, and he must use them.

Back at camp he made a quick supper of bacon and biscuits and coffee, and afterward sat back on his tarp, his back against a tree, and watched evening come to the meadows. Tomorrow, he would take this bunch down to the home ranch, and return for the rest, and this week would find his bunch together. Afterward, he must tell Carrie of his decision to give up Saber, and he wondered what she would say.

He was pondering this when he saw the rider come out of the aspens and head across the meadow for his camp. It took him a few moments to identify the spare, sinewy figure of old Cass Hardesty, and he felt the caution gather in him, remembering Cass's part in the fight.

Cass crossed the creek, his horse kicking up ribbons of water that the dusk turned to pure silver as they rose and fell. Cass was one of the oldest Saber hands, a dour and taciturn man who, for all his surliness, had been kind enough to Frank in the past. The short pipe that barely cleared his heavy black mustaches and which was removed from his mouth only when he ate and slept, jutted straight out from his heavy jaw.

He reined in by the fire, and Frank, as custom dictated, said, "Light and eat, Cass," in no friendly voice.

"Sure you want me?" He was embarrassed, Frank saw.

At Frank's nod, Cass stepped out of the saddle and looked about him. His glance settled on the corral with its eighteen horses, and he looked over at Frank. "That's a man-killin' job. Why didn't you ask Jess for the loan of a couple of hands?"

"I guess you know."

"Yeah," Cass said slowly. "Like you said, Johnny talks too much." He reflected a moment and added, "We all should of waited."

Frank tossed him a cup and Cass, squatting before the fire, poured himself some coffee. Removing his pipe, he drank deeply of the scalding coffee and then exhaled and looked over at Frank.

"You're passin' up a pretty good thing in Saber—if you are passin' it up."

"I am," Frank said.

Cass drank the rest of the coffee and with a spare, thoughtful movement, he put his pipe back in his mouth. "Who killed him?" he asked abruptly.

"Take your choice."

Cass almost smiled then. "I wouldn't pick you," he said mildly. "Not even after the namin' Rob gave you."

Frank didn't comment. Now Cass reached into the edge of the fire, picked up a coal, and placed it in the bowl of his pipe, puffing the tobacco alight. Decades of blacksmithing had given Cass calluses on his big hands that had turned his skin into a black and leathery rind, impervious to heat. When he had his light, he tossed the coal back into the fire and observed dryly, "If there was a bastard in the bunkhouse that night, I'd say it was Rob, not you."

"So would I," Frank said woodenly.

"When you didn't kill Rob that night, I figured you never would," Cass said. "That's why Hannan's wrong when he suspects you."

"How'd you know he does?"

"He said so," Cass replied. "He was out yesterday."

Frank felt a faint chill of premonition. Nunnally was at work, then.

"He wants you to come in and see him," Cass added, and now he looked at Frank. "That why you gave up Saber?"

Frank nodded. Cass stood up now and said off-handedly, "We figured a week ago you'd come back and rooster around, maybe pension Jess off and fire the whole bunch of us that heard Rob name you."

"How do you know I wouldn't have, if Hannan had let me alone?"

"You could have kept the outfit long enough to fire us, couldn't you?"

Frank remained silent, wondering what this was leading up to, and Cass seemed satisfied. He took his pipe out of his mouth and looked at it, scowling, and then he said, almost shyly: "Johnny saw some of your ponies over by the Horn Creek line camp last week. He'll drive 'em over tomorrow. You go on down and see Hannan, and Johnny and me will bring down your string."

Frank stared at him uncomprehendingly, and Cass met his glance. Finally, Frank asked, "Why, Cass?"

"Damned if I rightly know," Cass murmured. "For ten years I watched Rob kick you into somethin' I didn't much like. And then, when you're finally rid of him, Hannan tries it. That's too much." He paused. "Can Johnny and me help?"

"Sure," Frank said softly.

Next morning at daybreak Frank turned his string of horses out of the corral, and he and Cass ran them for a couple of miles until the edge was off them. Cass turned back then, and Frank made the drive alone down to Saber, which he reached at midday.

Turning the bunch into the big corral at Saber, he held them long enough to rope out a close-coupled bay and change his saddle to him, after which he turned the remainder into the horse pasture.

Riding past the cookshack he got a reluctant wave from the cook standing in the doorway, and that was all.

He made the ride down to Rifle at a mile-eating walk and jog, and now he speculated on what Hannan, prompted by Hugh's misinformation, might say to him. Anything could happen; he didn't know. In late afternoon he came to the break in the timber on the grade above Rifle. Below him, and downriver, he could see the town and the crawling antlike figures making up the traffic in the main street.

Off toward the river below town, he heard faint shouts and whistles. Raising his glance, he saw a band of horses being hazed out of Rhino's horse lot and downriver by a trio of riders. The uniform solid color of every horse told him what he wanted to know. This was part of the bunch he and Hugh had brought in from Utah—all solid color, all under sixteen hands high, all flat-backed and close-coupled geldings between six and nine years old. They met the requirements of the United States Cavalry, and were now being driven downriver on the way to Fort Crawford, a hundred and twenty miles away. He remembered the long drive through the desert to Crawford that he had made in early summer for Rhino, and he was glad he was not with them.

Rifle's main street, when he came into it later, was busy with late afternoon traffic. A five-team hitch on a big corn wagon just unloaded at Rhino's was hauled up in front of the Pleasant Hour. A half-dozen kids were playing noisily in the high-sided empty wagon, and as Frank pulled in at the hotel tie-rail Barney Josephson came out of his saddle shop across the street to quiet them lest they stampede the half-broken teams.

Frank dismounted at the tie-rail of the Colorado House on the corner opposite the brick bank. The usual row of idlers in their barrel chairs on the boardwalk in front of the hotel windows regarded him curiously, some nodding to him. He went past them into the lobby and was making for the desk when he saw Hannan in the far corner of the lobby. The sheriff was alone, seated in a deep leather chair under a motheaten mounted elk head, and in his hand was what looked to Frank like a slim whalebone corset stay. Frank halted and watched him a moment in curious puzzlement. Suddenly, Hannan flicked the corset stay at his knee. A faint smile of satisfaction appeared around the cold cigar in his mouth. He flicked again at the arm of the chair, and then Frank understood. Hannan was swatting flies.

As Frank approached, Hannan looked up. He didn't rise, didn't offer to shake hands, only said mildly, "Hello, Frank," as he tucked the stay back in the inside pocket of his coat.

Frank said, "Hello, Buck. How's the hunting?"

"They're hard to hit," Hannan observed tranquilly. He re-

41

garded Frank a moment and said, "Who pasted that black eye on you?"

"Nobody you have to worry about, Buck." Frank sat on the arm of a near-by chair and came directly to the point. "They said you were looking for me."

"Worried?"

Frank nodded. "Some. I'd like to know where I stand."

"A little closer to a trial than you did a couple days ago," Hannan observed. He chewed thoughtfully on his cigar before he said, "I suppose your memory is a sorry thing."

"Memory of what?"

"You wouldn't, for instance, know where you were the five days between the Fourth of July and the ninth, would you? Do you recollect anybody shootin' anvils, or celebrating the Fourth?"

Frank's face went bland and blank. "No. I didn't carry a calendar, Buck. I don't remember."

"I thought so. You remember a man named Booker?"

"Should I?"

"You bought five horses from him on the Fourth. You remember a man name of Headly? No, of course you don't. You bought eight horses from him on the ninth."

"Who said I did?"

"Nunnally," Hannan said. "I been checking dates on bills of sale with him. He claims you bought horses from both Booker and Headly on those dates and turned the bills of sale over to him. He can't recollect your buying any in between those dates. Can you?"

Frank didn't answer immediately. Almost imperceptibly, Nunnally was drawing the noose tighter, and there was nothing he could do to stop it. If he contradicted this latest fiction of Hugh's, Hannan would make him prove the contradiction. He said now, "Where did I run across Booker and Headly?"

"Around Moab."

"That would give me time to leave Booker, ride here for Rob, track him down, kill him, and get back in time to buy Headly's horses on the ninth. That what you're thinking, Buck?"

"You said it, I didn't," Hannan observed dryly. He was watching Frank closely.

"Have you and Doc Breathit decided when Rob was killed? What date?"

"The last time he was seen was on the Fourth. He picked up a drunk O-Bar puncher that night and put him back on his horse, the puncher says."

"And why did I kill him?" Frank murmured.

"You hated him."

"Did *you* like him?" Frank countered. "Can you find me anybody who did?"

"That's different."

"No," Frank said flatly. "Ever since I was ten I've been mad enough at Rob to kill him. Lots of times. But I never did. Why should I sneak back from Utah to do it?"

"He said some pretty hard things about your mother the night you left, so I hear."

Frank nodded. "Hard enough things so I could have pulled a gun on him and killed him then, and nobody would have blamed me. But I didn't."

Hannan said nothing, only studied Frank's face.

Now Frank said, "That reason is no good, Buck. What others have you got?"

"There's Saber. You got that."

"And I'm not taking it," Frank said slowly. "Not until you find Rob's killer. If you never do, I never take Saber."

Hannan sighed and said, "Yeah, I heard about that at Saber." He reached in his pocket and pulled out the corset stay. There was a fly on his pants leg, and he flicked at it viciously. The fly fell to the floor and did not move, and Hannan moodily returned the corset stay to his pocket. Then he said worriedly, "You got me there, Frank."

"Then let me alone," Frank said flatly.

Something in his voice made Hannan look up, and Frank rose.

"I mean it, Buck," Frank said.

Hannan sighed and rubbed his chin and said, in an almost inaudible voice, "I know you do."

Frank went out through the lobby then, and on the boardwalk he paused and rolled a cigarette. His hands, he noticed, were shaking. How well had he succeeded in checking Hannan? There was no way of telling except that, by his own admission, he couldn't offer a reason for Rob's murder by Frank. Frank took a deep drag of his cigarette now and contemplated the next move. He might as well see Judge Tavister and get the Saber business over with. He waited until a team pulling a buckboard passed him, then crossed to the opposite corner and took the stairway that mounted to the second floor of the brick bank.

Judge Tavister's office was the corner one, and looking down the corridor through the open door, Frank saw him seated at his desk talking to someone whom Frank could not see.

Approaching the door now, Frank saw the Judge was talking with Carrie. She was sitting on his desk amid a scattering of papers, her feet swinging, and when Frank appeared in the door, her face lighted up. She was dressed in a long-sleeved street dress of green and gray bombazine. When she looked at Frank's face, however, her feet which had been swinging against the desk, became motionless.

She said slowly, "Who've you been fighting with?"

Frank only grinned and shook his head. Judge Tavister was regarding him without any cordiality in his face. He gestured toward a chair which Frank, after placing his hat on the long table, dragged up. Carrie slipped down off the desk, and coming up beside him, touched his eye tenderly. There was a look of silent reproof in her face, Frank noticed.

Judge Tavister said, "Come about the business?"

At Frank's nod the Judge rose, opened the cabinet beside his desk, and took several papers out and laid them on the table, swiveling his chair around to face the table too.

"Want me out, Dad?" Carrie asked.

"Don't go," Frank said. "It'll save me telling you, Carrie." He looked at the Judge. "I don't want Saber for a while, Judge. How do you go about putting it away?"

There was a long silence, and then Carrie echoed, "Don't want Saber?"

Frank nodded, not looking at her. "Hannan seems to think I killed Rob," he said. "He thinks I did it because I wanted Saber. I'd like to put Saber away until he's found Rob's killer. If he doesn't find him, I don't want it."

Judge Tavister could not hide the distress in his face, but before he had a chance to speak Carrie said hotly, "That fat fool of a Hannan! I'll kill him!"

"Now, now, don't say that even in fun, Carrie," her father admonished.

"But it's blackmail!" Carrie said hotly.

Judge Tavister looked at Frank now. "That's absurd, Frank. The property is legally yours. Let Hannan try and make a case against you."

"He can't, if I don't take Saber."

Carrie said indignantly, "But what about you? You give up a big ranch!"

The Judge said temperately: "Exactly. You're doing it backwards, Frank. Our law is founded on the assumption that a man is innocent until proven guilty; not that he is guilty until proven innocent—as you seem to believe. Let Hannan prove it."

Frank said dismally, "What if he can make out a good case?"

"How can he? Can't you account for your time?"

"No," Frank lied.

"Weren't you traveling with Rhino's men?"

"Not all the time," he lied again.

A look of bitter accusation mounted in Judge Tavister's eyes, and Frank knew what he was thinking. This was the "hurt" he mentioned that night in the quiet darkness, the disgrace shaping up that would break Carrie's heart, and Frank saw the Judge understand this and accept it with a wry dislike. The Judge said stonily: "It's yours to dispose of, Frank. I'm Rob's executor. I suppose I could arrange to put Saber in escrow under the terms you wish."

Carrie looked from Frank now to her father, and the protest mounted in her green eyes and she looked levelly at Frank. "So all you said the other night was fluff? You said you'd run Saber and prove to me you weren't a drifter, that you'd accept that responsibility, didn't you?"

Frank nodded miserably.

"And now you won't. You've seen a chance to dodge and duck again."

"What am I dodging?" Frank asked wearily.

"You have a chance at last!" Carrie said passionately. "You've got a ranch to run, a crew to pay, cattle to raise and ship! You've—you've even got a wife to win—if you want her!"

Frank looked down at his hands a long moment, and he tasted the full bitterness of this. The one thing that could free him he could not tell her, because in telling her he would lose her.

He rose now and shook his head and said miserably, "You've got to let me work it out my way, Carrie."

"Yes," Carrie said quietly. She managed a faint and unenthusiastic smile. "Maybe a few more months added onto six years won't kill me. But you can't dodge forever, Frank."

She came up to him then, raised on tiptoe and kissed him. "There. I've stopped scolding."

Afterward, Frank went down the stairs and turned aimlessly into the street, a gray despair riding him. Carrie was still loyal to him, but he had disappointed her again, and this time deeply. The most he could hope for was time, time in which to prove to her that he would work at other things, if not at Saber.

He found himself teetering on the edge of the boardwalk, staring blankly at the hotel across the street. A sudden hunger moved him into the street, headed him for the hotel dining room—a slim-hipped, restless man with misery in his face.

Chapter 7

Hugh Nunnally drifted into the lobby of the Colorado House and idled up to the desk. He said good evening to Mr. Newhouse, the owner, bought a couple of cigars at the counter by the desk, and then strolled over to one of the deep leather chairs and sat down. Passing the dining room, he didn't even bother to look in. He knew Frank was there.

He lighted a cigar, stretched out his legs, and settled himself comfortably. Isaac Maas, the owner of the *Rifle Tribune* down the street, spoke to him with his customary gentleness on his way into the dining room, and Hugh lazily waved in answer. Afterward, he studied the half-dozen mounted elk and deer heads on the far wall, idly counting the points on each pair of antlers and wondering if he had killed bigger. There was nothing much on his mind; he had gone over what needed going over.

Presently, Frank Chess came out of the dining room. Hugh, unobserved, watched him, noting the black eye and marked nose and the sober set to his dark, alert face, and he smiled. Rising, Hugh strolled over to the dining room door, looked inside, verified what he already knew, and then came back through the lobby.

Through the front window, he saw Frank just touching a light to his cigarette. Hugh reached the door just as Frank was untying the reins of his horse at the hotel tie-rail, and Hugh strolled across the boardwalk and put a shoulder against the veranda pillar.

"Nice horse, Frank," he observed. "Want to sell him?"

Frank looked up, and a hard scowl came on his face. "Not to you."

Hugh smiled and said pleasantly, "Rhino'd like to see you."

Frank had his foot in the stirrup. He paused and looked sharply at Nunnally, and Hugh could almost see him telling himself, *Maybe I'd better.*

Frank said derisively, "You're a big fella now, Hugh. Why don't you quit running errands for him?"

Nunnally wasn't to be baited; he smiled faintly. "I don't mind it. Coming?"

Frank tied his reins again while Hugh skirted the tie-rail, and fell in beside him. They crossed the street, passed the bank, and beyond it turned into Willie Haver's barbershop. Haver, a bald, slight little man, was seated in one of his two chairs reading a worn paper, and at their entrance he lifted his thumb and pointed over his shoulder toward the rear and resumed his reading.

In the corridor Hugh, leading the way, again smiled faintly, this time in anticipation. He palmed open the knob of the second door and stepped inside. This was a big, dimly lit room, the left rear corner of it filled with an oversize zinc bathtub. Rhino Hulst lay half-submerged in its soapy water, a half-smoked cigar in his mouth, a folded newspaper in one hand. There was a wall lamp behind and above him which was lighted against the perpetual gloom of this warm, soapy-smelling room. Rhino's massive arms and chest almost filled the width of the tub. Beside him on the floor stood a brace of buckets filled with hot water.

Rhino didn't even look at Hugh, who crossed the room to the back wall.

"Hello, son," Rhino said pleasantly to Frank.

"Hello, Uncle Rhino," Frank said mockingly.

47

Hugh, seating himself in a straight-backed chair, felt a perverse pleasure in Frank's cockiness. It would make what followed so much more entertaining. He put his elbows on his knees and looked up at Rhino in time to see him scowling.

"Is it the light, or have you got a black eye?" Rhino inquired mildly.

Hugh looked over at Frank and saw that he had put his shoulders against the front wall, and tucked his thumbs in the pockets of his pants.

"Get down to business, Fatty," Frank murmured.

Rhino chuckled. "How do you like Hannan's theory?" Rhino asked. "I don't see how you can beat it."

"I've already beat it," Frank said.

"Giving up Saber?" Rhino asked mildly. He shook his head. "Won't do you much good, I'm afraid, Frank."

Frank, Hugh saw, was faintly surprised that Rhino knew of this. Frank touched a match to his cold cigarette, and then looked idly at it. "How far are you going with this, Rhino?" he asked then.

"Right up to the finish."

"I won't hang for Rob's murder. The finish will be me telling Hannan about the uniform so he can prove where I was."

Nunnally cut in softly, "You're lying," and watched the caution come into Frank's dark eyes. He went on, still softly, "You want that girl too badly, Frank, and she won't have you, knowing that about you."

"You'd hate to bet on that, wouldn't you, Hugh?"

"I have bet on it," Rhino put in calmly. "That uniform can get me in trouble too, but not as much as it can you. I'm betting you'll never tell Hannan."

Frank's eyes widened. "I'd hang first?"

Rhino shook his head in negation. "You'll come back first. That's what I'm trying to tell you. It's the only way out."

Hugh watched stubbornness come into Frank's handsome face, darkening it, and he felt return of the same perverse pleasure. There was nothing complicated about Chess, he thought; like a hooked fish, there were only so many motions he could go through, variations on the same protest, before he subsided.

"I won't come back, Rhino," Frank said flatly, angrily. "I've worn that uniform for the last time."

"Of course you have," Rhino agreed mildly. "Who said anything about a uniform?"

"Hugh."

Rhino glanced reprovingly at Hugh, who was studying the floor now, seemingly out of this.

"Hugh has my interests at heart," Rhino said forgivingly. "He was just trying to drive the cheapest bargain." Now Rhino puffed on his cigar long enough to find it had gone out. He tossed it carelessly onto the floor, and then said, almost idly, "No, what I had in mind was a partnership, Frank."

Hugh looked up in time to catch the surprise in Frank's face. "Partnership?" Frank echoed blankly.

"In Saber," Rhino said. He settled back in the tub a little, laced his fingers together behind his neck and looked at the ceiling a moment, and then frowned. Looking at Hugh now, he said, "Get me a cigar, Hugh, and warm this water for me, will you?"

Hugh went over to the chair where Rhino's clothes were lying, took a cigar from the breast pocket of Rhino's coat, gave it to him, held a match for the cigar, then dumped one of the buckets of water into the tub. Occasionally, as he moved about this business, he glanced at Frank, and reading what he saw in Frank's face he thought, *He's quick enough. He knows.*

He came back to his chair and sat down, and now Rhino said with a gentle persuasiveness: "Look how it is. I've got money and plenty of horse-buyers, but every time the Army needs a big jag of horses I have to go buy them. You've got Saber, the buildings, the grass. Together, we could raise horses, buy them, hold them, trade them and sell them. We'd be the biggest horse-dealers in the West. Why, we'd make a fortune."

Frank had come away from the wall now. His dark eyes were bright and steady and remotely searching as he regarded Rhino.

Then he said softly, "Rhino, you killed Rob, didn't you?"

Rhino chuckled. "Why, yes."

Hugh gently slipped his gun from its holster and held it beside him. He watched Frank accept this, standing utterly motionless, his lean restlessness stilled, hands at his side, feet spread a little apart, his face hard and unforgiving and strangely wild.

Frank's glance shuttled to Hugh now, and Hugh said dryly, "Do you care?"

Afterward, there was a full half-minute of silence. Frank balled up his right fist and rubbed it gently in the palm of his left hand, and he stared at the floor. Hugh watched him a tense ten seconds and then he thought, *He'll take it,* and relaxed, waiting for the rest.

Rhino said presently, "Now, Frank, listen carefully. There are three things you can do." He leaned both arms on the edge of the tub and waggled an admonitory finger at Frank. "You can get reckless and walk out of here straight to Hannan and tell him I've just said I killed Rob. If you do, I won't even have to deny it. I'll simply tell Hannan you came to me with the proposition to split Saber with me if I would dig up a man who could prove you were with him between the fourth and ninth of July. Hugh will be my witness. Furthermore, after Hannan's arrested you, I'll dig up a man who *saw* you *here* between the fourth and ninth."

Rhino paused, nodded as if to nail this down, and then touched the second finger of his left hand, ticking off the second item. "Or," he said, "you can free yourself of all suspicion of Rob's murder by telling Hannan you were wearing an Army uniform between the fourth and the ninth." He smiled at the idiocy of this suggestion.

"Or," he continued, spreading his hands, "you can get Saber back, throw in with me, and I'll prove you were with my crew between the fourth and the ninth. After that, we'll make money."

He settled back in the bathtub, although Hugh heard this rather than saw it. He was watching the gathering wildness in Frank's face, and he thought resignedly, *Here we go.*

Frank turned and moved toward the door, and Hugh rose and said sharply, "What'll it be, Frank?"

"I'm going to Hannan," Frank said.

Hugh tipped up his gun and said, "Stay there," and Frank halted. Carefully, Hugh moved over to him and lifted the gun from the waistband of Frank's levis, and then stepped back.

Rhino said mildly, "Are you sure, Frank?"

Frank didn't answer. Hugh glanced over at Rhino, saw Rhino's nod, and then he hefted Frank's gun in his hand, cocking it. Once it was cocked, he pointed it at the floor and pulled the trigger. The shot bellowed through the room, and Hugh, still keeping Frank covered, moved over to the door and opened it and called sharply, "Willie! Get Hannan at the hotel!"

He heard Willie run out, and now he looked at Frank and grinned lazily. "Begin to shape up?" he asked gently.

"You're a fool, Frank," Rhino said crossly.

They waited then, and Hugh watched the bitter resignation replace the anger in Frank's eyes.

When, some minutes later, Buck Hannan hurried through the door, they were standing exactly as they had been. Buck halted just inside the room and looked from one to the other. Willie Haver and a couple of men poked their heads into the room, but Rhino shouted angrily, "Get out, you fools! I'm taking a bath!"

Hannan closed the door on the curious, and then said to Rhino, "What's the trouble, Rhino?" He eyed Frank with a cold suspicion, Hugh noticed.

Hugh handed him Frank's gun, and then Rhino said, "Look, Buck. Isn't there any way you can keep this wild man off my back?" in a plaintive, half-angry tone.

Hannan looked again at Frank and said softly, "Sure. What happened?"

"He shot at me," Rhino said. "That is, he was going to, if Hugh hadn't knocked his gun down."

"Why?" Hannan demanded.

Rhino glanced levelly at Frank and said, "You feel like telling him, Chess?" His voice held an undertone of irony.

Frank's face was stony and expressionless. Hugh saw him take a deep breath, saw his lips part, as if he were going to speak, and then his lips closed. He said nothing, didn't even shake his head, and Hugh smiled faintly, derisively, thinking, *He's folded.*

"All right," Rhino said resignedly. "Hugh brought him here because he asked to see me. He boiled in here and said he'd heard Virg Moore was coming in from Utah and to keep him out of town."

"Who's Virg Moore?" Hannan asked quickly.

"One of my crew," Rhino said patiently. "I've sent for him, already, but Chess didn't like it. When I told him I couldn't stop Virg coming, he said Virg would lie about where he was between the fourth and ninth, and he pulled a gun on me. Hugh jumped him, and Frank's gun went off."

Hannan raised the gun and smelled it, and then said coldly to Frank, "That what happened?"

"No."

"What did?"

Frank looked wickedly at the four of them, and said tonelessly, "Anything they say."

Hannan said dryly, "For a man that couldn't have killed Rob, you seem pretty damn jumpy." He glanced now at Rhino. "What do you want me to do? Arrest him for attempted murder? You'll have to complain first, Rhino."

"What about a peace bond?" Nunnally suggested gently.

"No, no," Rhino protested. "Hell, I don't want to persecute him. The kid's worried, and I don't blame him. Maybe Virg will lie. But I can't have him shooting at me."

"Well, what do you want me to do?" Hannan demanded in exasperation. "Scold him?"

Rhino said crossly, "Oh, hell, forget it, Buck; I was scared, that's all."

Hannan wheeled on Frank now, and Hugh saw the anger in the sheriff's face. Hannan said mockingly, savagely, " 'Let me alone,' eh? I'll let you alone, Chess, when you can account for every minute between the fourth and the ninth—every damn minute!" He strode to the door and paused. "When Virg Moore comes in, send him straight to me."

He went out, absently taking Frank's gun with him.

When Hannan had gone, Nunnally, grinning broadly, looked over at Rhino.

Rhino's face had dropped its geniality now. He looked at Frank closely and said, "You had your chance. Where was your story to Hannan?"

A slow flush crept into Frank's face, and the look of baleful anger in his eyes stirred Rhino into irritation.

"I can do anything with you I want, can't I? Tell any story I want, can't I, as long as you're afraid of that soldier suit?"

When Frank didn't answer, Rhino said crisply: "Virg will be here in five days. You better see me before he gets here. Now get out."

Chapter 8

TESS LET HERSELF into her room with the key and crossed to the window and opened it. The late afternoon sun streamed cheerfully into the room, filtering through the bright curtains, but as Tess stood in the window, looking out over the back lots and rooftops of the town, she could not rid herself of the depression that had been with her all day. She stared at the roofs, trying to imagine this another town, wishing desperately that it were and that she did not have to go through the next hour.

Presently, she turned and walked over to the mirror above the washstand and looked at herself. *I make a handsome executioner,* she thought, and the absurdity of it brought a smile to her face. She was, she knew, being too tragic about this; the world wouldn't end however it turned out, and it was time she learned to compromise.

She unbuttoned her drab office dress, stepped out of it, and with a grimace of distaste, hung it in her tiny closet, exchanging it for a plain blue dress starched so stiffly it rustled when she moved it.

Dressed in it, she took down a small hat and, taking a last look in the mirror, let herself out. Carrying her hat, she went down into the lobby, leaving the key at the desk. The usual bunch of lobby loafers eyed her approvingly, and she was aware of this and even enjoyed it. On the boardwalk, she turned left and took the side street toward the river. The boardwalk gave out two doors past the hotel, and as she stepped onto the weed-grown cinder path along the road, she could see the McGarritys' wagon yard ahead, with the single spreading cottonwood above it. Surrounding it was a new slab fence, and the sight of it touched her strangely. Slab was cheap; Moffat's sawmill gave it away for a few cents a hundred feet, and the McGarritys, with seldom a spare dollar, had used it for all their buildings and fence.

The office was on the road, and approaching it Tess heard a hostler in the back lot cursing a horse with passionate profanity.

She hoped that it wasn't Jonas or John McGarrity. They were shy enough normally.

She entered the open door of the office and looked around her. Jonas McGarrity was looking out the high scales window in the back wall, his elbows resting on the sill. There was a battered desk in the corner, and John McGarrity, neat as always in his black suit, had his feet on it.

Jonas called out the window then, "Kick him in the belly, Gus."

At the same moment, John McGarrity caught sight of Tess, and he came crashingly to his feet. Jonas turned now, and seeing Tess, a deep crimson flush mounted to his morose face.

Tess laughed. "Don't mind, boys, I hear that all day."

Jonas grinned sheepishly. "I guess we're not used to women around, Tess."

John shoved his chair toward Tess and she sat down. Catching the worried look in his round face, she said impulsively, "I'm not on a dunning job, boys, so don't look so worried."

John looked at Jonas and laughed. "It's a good thing, Tess. We won't collect on that job yesterday for another two weeks."

He pulled up a rough deal chair and Jonas folded his long legs to sit on the slab bench against the wall. Tess looked around the office and said, "I wish I had this much room. And scales, too."

Jonas scratched his head and said, "I don't, ma'am. You'd have all the business."

They all smiled at this, and Tess's heart sank. How was she going to break the news she must? These men liked her, and she liked them, and there was no way to sugarcoat this pill.

She began, then, at the beginning, telling of her submission of her monthly report to Rhino, and of his calling her in and complimenting her. As the story unfolded, Jonas gave one puzzled, confounded glance at John, and then returned his attention to her. When she finished by relating that Rhino had ordered her to get their price for the whole outfit, John sat utterly still a moment. He rose slowly then, rubbed the back of his neck with the palm of his hand and circled the room.

He came to a stop before her and said quietly. "You know how we're fixed, Tess. We can't buck you."

"Not her; Rhino," Jonas amended gloomily.

"Of course," John said absently. He smiled politely, and Tess felt a twinge of pain. The two brothers stared at each other silently, and Tess knew they wanted to be alone to talk this over. Yet there was something she must say too, and now she murmured, "Then why buck him?"

Jonas frowned. "You mean we ought to sell out to him at his price?"

"Never," Tess said flatly. "That's what he's depending on. Just forget yourselves for a moment and think of him. I've already chosen an agent in Leadville and written to him, with instructions to advertise our new low rates. What will happen next?"

"Shippers will leave us for you," John said.

"And we can't handle it," Tess said. "We haven't the wagons or the teams or the teamsters. It means we'll have to buy a lot of new equipment at a top price."

"So Rhino does," John said. "What then?"

"I'm not sure he does," Tess said slowly. "He's counting on your selling to him. If he has to buy new equipment and then keep losing money on his low rates because you're waiting to jump in with all your equipment, he'll give it up."

"Are you sure of that, Tess?" John asked soberly.

Tess shook her head in negation. "No. I'm just counting on his greed."

John looked at Jonas, and Jonas said bitterly, "That don't feed us, Tess—holding on waiting for him to quit."

"Then hurry him up," Tess said vehemently. "Quote me a silly figure of a hundred thousand dollars for your equipment. Board up your windows, lock your gate, insure your wagons, and drive your horses into the mountains. Get a job on round-up, or go hunting. Live on beans or deermeat, and don't come back till the snow drives you in." She smiled wryly. "By that time, our wagons will be wrecked, we'll have a dozen suits for non-delivery of freight on our hands, and I'll be taking up all his time with complaints. Either that, or we'll have new wagons, and our rates will have gone up so high you can cut under us."

The two brothers looked at each other a long moment, and then John cleared his throat. "Tess, you mind if Jonas and me step out a minute?"

"I'll go," Tess said, beginning to rise.

John said hurriedly: "No. Please don't. It won't take a minute."

Tess settled back in her chair, and Jonas followed John out the side door. She could hear an indistinct muttering then, and low serious answers.

Well, I've done it and I feel cleaner, she thought. This decision had come hard to her, for she was by nature a loyal person, and she knew what she had just done was disloyal to Rhino. He had befriended her after her father's death and given her work, and she had appreciated that. But this that he had ordered her to do had no bearing on that obligation, she felt. She would carry out orders and work as faithfully as she could for him. Would it then be her fault if the McGarritys defeated her, and through her, Rhino, in the end? She didn't think so.

She was wondering, a small doubt still within her, when she heard footsteps outside and turned her head. Frank Chess stepped through the doorway, and when he caught sight of her, he halted.

His swift grin came only fleetingly from behind some deep restlessness in him, and he said reprovingly, "You're in Indian country, Tess."

Tess could feel the color come into her face, and she said quickly, "It's just business."

Frank looked curiously at her, and at that moment John and Jonas came in. Tess noticed oddly that a subtle change came into the faces of the brothers as they saw Frank, and she remembered seeing it before on the faces of other men when they saw him. It was as if he touched everyone with a kind of happy-go-lucky friendliness that had a small magic in it. It seemed as if it had never occurred to him that he could not like everybody, and that everybody could not like him, so they did.

Frank said, "I've got those two teams for you, John, and I'll trade any part of them for a buckboard. Have you got a buckboard?"

"How long does it have to hold together?" Jonas asked. "We got a wreck out there, Frank."

"I'll take it," Frank said promptly. "I've got to get it to Saber tonight, though. Got a team free you can loan me? I'll have them and four good horses back to you tomorrow."

"Sure," John said. He looked at Jonas inquiringly, and then

back at Frank. "About those teams, Frank. We won't need them." And then, as if he did not want his refusal to sound unkind, he added quickly, "We're closing up the yard at the end of the week."

Tess felt a sobering pride then; they trusted her good faith enough to take her advice. She saw the look of puzzlement on Frank's face, and now Jonas observed, not without bitterness in his voice, "Rhino's decided to retire us."

Frank glanced quizzically at Tess now, and John said quickly, "No fault of Tess's. She's helped us."

Jonas walked to the scales window now and called out to a hostler to hitch up the buckboard, and then he came back to Tess. "Our price," he said to her with a wry solemnity, "is a hundred and fifty thousand. Make it in two checks, please."

Tess smiled a little, but it really wasn't something to joke about. John came over now and said in a low tone, "If this got out, Tess, it could go rough with you, couldn't it?" When Tess nodded, John said, "Shall I ask Frank to forget it?"

"I'll talk to him," Tess said, and she rose. Frank had moved over to the scales window and was looking out into the yard. She surprised a bitter, faraway look in his face that stirred her strangely before he realized she was beside him and turned.

"There's no moon, and you aren't asking me," Tess said quietly, "but I'd like a small ride in your new buckboard, Frank."

He remembered, she saw; he gave her a slow, quizzical smile and said, "All right, Tess."

Afterward, the buckboard came, and Jonas helped her up while Frank held the team. She said good-bye soberly to the McGarritys, and Frank put the team in motion, turning down toward the river road.

The dusty road along the river under the cottonwoods was somehow peaceful and deceptively remote from town, and the smooth oily sound of the river's rush beside and below them was almost hypnotic. Tess listened to it, covertly watching Frank, studying him now with a close and critical appraisal. Even with a black eye, whose origin teased her curiosity, he was wholly handsome in a way that was exciting and disturbing to her, and there was a careless, friendly charm about him that was as unconscious to him as his breathing.

She wondered at the present grimness of his face, but she

knew that would not last, for there was a deep and irrepressible gaiety of spirit in him that would not be downed, and which touched a fondness deep in herself. She knew of his life, of his bitter quarrels with Rob Custis, and of the wild and reckless and fun-loving way he had about him. Most people, she noticed, openly liked him, but the sober among them held him in a half-derisive affection that she was shrewd enough to understand and discount. They mistrusted their instinct to like him, perhaps remembering the fable of the ant and the grasshopper. But Tess knew that while the industrious ant disapproved of the idle grasshopper, he was nevertheless willing to eat him, and that envy and faded hopes and small disappointments were behind that derision.

Remembering her purpose now, she stirred herself and said quietly, "Have you put everything together about me and the McGarritys, Frank?"

"I'm not supposed to, am I?" he asked slowly.

Tess told him of her errand then, and she found herself wanting desperately to convince him of the rightness of her decision. As she told him of Rhino's design to ruin the McGarritys, a grim smile flicked faintly at the corner of his mouth. When she finished telling him of the McGarritys' decision to take her advice about closing, he was silent a long minute, and she watched him obliquely, waiting.

"That's good advice. What's worrying you?" he asked then. "Me?"

"No, only Rhino's been good to me," Tess said hesitantly, feeling for the right words. "I feel disloyal to him—a little."

Frank looked straight ahead as he said, "Would you rather live with that, or with the memory of keeping quiet while he strangled them?"

"With that, if I have to live with either."

"You shouldn't have to live with either," Frank said musingly, "but that's what Rhino does to you." He looked at her now. "Why are you working for him?"

The transition between the two questions was too abrupt for her, and Tess was silent a moment. This was her first hint that someone else had seen Rhino as she did, and she wanted to ask questions. The chance was past, though, and now she answered his other question.

"Loyalty again. He gave me work so I wouldn't have to live on Judge Tavister's charity."

Frank turned his face full to her now, and there was a look of astonishment there. "Tavister?"

"Yes. Dad was a teamster for Rhino until he was hurt. Then he was driver and handyman for Judge Tavister until he died. Afterward, the Judge asked Rhino to take me in, and he did."

"But where was I?" Frank demanded.

"Drifting."

Frank looked sharply at her, and Tess said quietly, "Would you rather I put it another way? I don't like that word, myself."

"No, that word will do," Frank said soberly, and he returned his gaze to the road. Tess had a feeling she had trespassed on something she did not understand, and she was speculating on this when Frank asked idly, "Did Carrie like you?"

It was her turn now to be astonished, and now he looked at her with a mocking, friendly curiosity. "I don't think so," she said then. "If she remembers at all, she'll tell you she didn't like it when I wouldn't take the room she'd arranged for me with a nice family. I wanted to live in the hotel."

"Why did she want you to take a room?"

Tess shrugged, amused by his curiosity. "The right men would call on me there. I'd be in the right house. After the right amount of courting I would have the right husband."

"And you didn't want one?"

Tess said, without hesitation: "The husband, yes. The careful waiting, no." She laughed a little. "I like to sit in the hotel lobby and talk with drummers and hear what's going on over the pass. I like to play poker with Mr. Newhouse and Doc Breathit and Mr. Maas. I like to drink a beer with old John Colby the nights he isn't driving stage. I like to go way up to the dances at the Horn Creek schoolhouse with some homely puncher and get home at dawn. I make a pretty poor lady, I guess."

"No," Frank said dryly, "you just won't try to be one."

Tess laughed. "Maybe that's it."

They smiled at each other in strange communion and afterward Tess remembered this.

The river road came into the main road now, and Frank swung the buckboard back toward town. They were both silent now, and Tess felt a pleasant contentment. She had needed that spare and offhand reassurance that he had given her, and later when she was alone, she could ponder his reference to Rhino.

In the middle of the business block, Tess said, "Let me down at the *Tribune*, Frank."

Frank pulled up the team in front of the newspaper office and glanced at its dark interior. "You're too late, Tess."

"I have a key," Tess said.

At Frank's look of bewilderment she laughed. "I keep Mr. Maas's books for him. That's the way I get money to play poker with."

Frank looked at her a long moment, now soberly, and then he shook his head. "You're bad for me, Tess," he said, and afterward he smiled faintly to reassure her.

As she inserted the key in the door, she glanced up at the street, and saw Frank in front of the hotel tying his horse to the endgate of the buckboard. In the low sun, whose light lay cleanly on the quiet street, he seemed tall and spare and quick with a sure swiftness in his every movement. Remembering his parting words now, she was oddly disturbed.

Chapter 9

THE LONG AND UNACCUSTOMED DAY in the saddle yesterday, rounding up Frank's horses, had given Cass a restless night, so that he was thankful when his usual hour of arising came around, an hour before daylight. He pulled on his trousers, picked up his boots, went over to the cook's bunk and shook him, then passed softly on sock feet down the aisle between the rows of sleeping men. Outside, he put on his boots and took a look at the night, smelling the sweet chill of the coming morning.

Pouring a basin full of water, he bent over and washed. His big rough hands, gnarled and calloused, served as the goad to really awaken him as they passed over his seamed face. He scrubbed at his mustache until it was soft and silky, washed his bald head, dried himself, and then automatically reached for his pipe.

Loading it by feel with a shaggy black tobacco, he only then noticed the lamp lighted in the main house. It had been so long since he had seen a light in that end of the big place that he puzzled for a moment before remembering Frank. Was the youngster just going to bed or just getting up?

Cass lighted his pipe and watched a minute, savoring the raw raking shock of the tobacco in his lungs. During this time he saw Frank pass back and forth between the lamp and the window several times. Cass strolled over to the yard fence and watched, but even this close Frank's movements made no sense.

Cass considered now. Four days ago, his antagonism to this young cub wouldn't have brought him as far as the fence. Now, however, he had made his offer of help and it had been accepted. He shoved open the gate and walked over to the outside of Frank's room and halted just outside the sill, silently regarding the lamplit scene before him.

Frank had a great coil of inch-and-a-half rope on the floor. Every eight feet of its length he was seizing to it with wet rawhide a three-inch iron ring. Finished with one ring, he coiled up the completed section and measured out another eight feet. He was working so intently that Cass watched two full minutes before he spoke.

"Ain't seen that rig used since the war," Cass observed.

Startled, Frank wheeled, and when he saw who it was a grin came to his face. "Want to splice the ring in the end, Cass?"

Cass came in. He picked up the lone ring bigger than the others and began to unravel the rope, observing, "Didn't know you youngsters knew about this." They worked in silence many minutes, during which Cass covertly regarded Frank. There was a certain grim temper in his normally cheerful face, and Cass wondered what had gone on with Hannan yesterday. Cass said presently, "How big a string you goin' to drive, Frank?"

"How many horses did you and Johnny round up?"

"Thirty-nine."

"Then I'll get forty out of your bunch and mine, with the culls out."

"Where you drivin' 'em to?" Cass went on.

"Fort Crawford."

Cass eyed him curiously. "You been there?"

"This summer."

"Then why don't you loose-herd 'em? It's wide open country, only a hundred and twenty miles."

Frank was sitting cross-legged on the floor. Now he let his hand fall to his lap and regarded Cass levelly. "I may be traveling at night. Then, there's a cranky purchasing quartermaster at Crawford, and I want my teams in good shape." He hesitated, Cass thought, before he said, "Another reason, too. This might wind up with a race."

"With who?"

"Rhino," Frank said grimly. He went to work again, and asked then, without looking up, "Want to take the wheelers, Cass?" He looked up with a wicked mischief in his eyes.

"Do you need me?"

"You, Johnny, Red, and Shields."

Cass thought a moment. "You settle it with Jess."

It was barely full light when they finished and lugged the gear down to the blacksmith shop on the other side of the big log barn.

The McGarritys' rickety buckboard stood in front of the shop's open door where Frank had left it last night. Briefly, Frank explained to Cass what he wanted done: hoops and double cover which he had bought in town last night after leaving Tess were to be put on the buckboard; a handbrake was to be rigged up; the free end of the rope was to be spliced into the buckboard's tongue; the buckboard was to be loaded with sacked oats, bed-rolls, and grub for three days. The triangle clanged for breakfast as he finished.

He stopped in at the cook shack and asked that Cass's breakfast be saved out, and it was the measure of Cass's influence here that the cook accepted the request without protest. Afterward, at the washbench, he doused cold water on his head. The shock of it wakened him, so that his sleepless night was forgotten, and he went in for breakfast.

This was his first appearance at Saber since the fight, and he spoke only to those who spoke to him. Cass had not spoken for the crew when he proffered help, and remembering this, Frank kept silent and aloof, but something was afoot and the crew knew it, for Cass's urgent hammering was threaded all through the meal, and Frank surprised an occasional speculative look in his direction. Breakfast finished, he tramped up to the office where Jess Irby held morning court and parceled out the work to the crew.

Jess, seated in his swivel chair, listened carefully while Frank made his request. Frank summed it up by saying, "This is a loan from you to me, Jess. If they come they're on my payroll, and ask them, don't order them—if you can spare them."

Jess nodded gravely. "They'll go and I can spare them."

Frank went out then past the dozen men idling at the office door with their first morning smoke. In the corral he caught and saddled his sorrel and rode out into the horse pasture. With the volunteer help of Ray Shields, the horse-wrangler, he spent a pleasant half-hour rounding up his fifty-odd horses and driving them into the big corral. When the sun topped the eastern peaks, its first touch was warm and pleasant, and he enjoyed the prospect of this job. At the big corral, he found a curious trio of the crew had halted to watch what was going on.

By the time he and Ray had cut out all the horses who were not solid-colored or who were over nine years old, and had turned them back into the pasture, there were a half-dozen of the crew lined atop the corral. Among them, Frank noticed, was Jess Irby, and Frank knew in their silent way they were measuring him, this time for his knowledge of the business he had told them would be his.

Johnny Samuels and Red Thornton climbed down from the rail saying they were willing to work for him, and Frank told them what he wanted.

Afterward, he took up his position in the small corral by the pasture gate, and as the horse-wrangler led the first horse out of the big corral past him, Frank was aware that Jess had moved over on the corral fence behind him. So, he noticed, had the others. This horse was a chestnut gelding whose coat glistened like burnished gold in the sun. Frank looked briefly at him and said, "Turn him out."

Red Thornton promptly objected. "Frank, I been usin' that horse and he's sound."

"He's fifteen-three high. The Army says fifteen-two, Red."

They knew now what he was doing, and while there were some good-natured murmurs of doubt nobody openly questioned him, and the chestnut was turned out. The next four horses were acceptable, and were turned into the holding corral adjoining. By now, a dozen of the crew were watching silently, and Frank knew they would be quietly and mercilessly critical. They knew horses; he would have to prove that he did.

Red Thornton led the fifth horse past him now. He was a close-coupled bay, compact as a cob of corn, with the flat shoulders and rounded breadbasket the Army coveted. Frank glanced once at him as he was walked by and said, "Turn him out, Red."

Jess Irby, from behind him, chuckled. "I'll fight you on him, Frank."

Frank shook his head. "Sweenied shoulder, Jess." He walked up to the horse and pointed to a faint flat depression in the smoothly bunched muscles of the right shoulder which indicated an atrophied muscle. "That'll get by the Army vet, but not a line officer."

Jess rubbed his chin and said nothing. The men grinned at him, and Jess smiled faintly, too shrewd to argue.

The crew was uncritical as he turned down the fifteenth horse for calf knees, which they could all see, and only Ray Shields protested stubbornly at the rejection of the twenty-fourth horse for being herring-gutted. "I'll buy that damn horse, I like his chest," Ray said, as he turned him out. The crew hooted good-naturedly.

The fortieth and last horse was a sorrel, bearing, as did all the others, the hilted Saber brand which was Frank's own, instead of the hiltless Saber which was the ranch brand. The sorrel was bright-eyed, alert, fat and sleek as a woodchuck from his mountain summer. The crew looked at him and there was a murmur of approval.

Frank, this time, watched the horse pass him and made no comment. He made a circle with his finger, and Johnny Samuels, who was herding him, turned him and led him back. "No, sir," Frank said then. "No quartermaster would pay for him."

A wave of protest came from the crew, and a sudden grin came to Frank's face. He shook his head and said, "Get down and look at him."

A half-dozen punchers climbed off the corral and formed a

loose circle around the sorrel. They regarded the horse in silence, and Johnny Samuels asked doubtfully, then, "Fifteen hands three?"

"Fifteen-two," Frank said.

They studied him some more in silence and Jess Irby remarked dryly, "He's handin' you taffy, Johnny. He'll take him."

They all looked at Frank, and Frank shook his head. "Capped hip." He touched the sorrel's left hipbone, which bore a faint depression in its curve. Sometime long ago, a fall had clipped the point of the hipbone, which was enough to disqualify him for a cavalry mount.

Johnny Samuels still looked doubtful; he walked behind the sorrel, bent his knees a little and sighted over his back. A baffled expression was in his face as he straightened and shook his head. "He's hip down, all right." He glanced over at Frank, and his grin now was friendly. "Don't you ever sell me a horse, Frank."

The crew laughed at that, and Frank joined them. He knew now the truce was over, and that he was accepted. This, and the fight, was the price of readmission to Saber.

Frank chose from the leftovers now the wheel team, and he and Johnny harnessed them and led them over to the buckboard and hooked them up. A saddle was thrown on the near horse of this team. The long rope, with its iron rings, was stretched out ahead of the buckboard's tongue. Two by two, the chosen horses were led out by their new six-foot rope halters and haltered, a pair to each ring, a horse on either side of the big rope. When the tenth pair, with the near horse also saddled, was brought out, it was put in harness, and a chain joined the inside hame of each; and the big rope laid over it to keep it from dragging the ground. Ten more pair of horses were haltered ahead of this team, and then the lead team was harnessed to the ring in the end of the rope.

Cass, when he finally stepped into the saddle of the near horse of the wheel team, could look over the backs of twenty-one teams stretched out a hundred and seventy feet ahead of him. The buckboard behind him, with its new snowy cover over the hoops, looked almost diminutive. Red Thornton climbed into the saddle of the near horse of the swing team. Johnny Samuels, on the near horse of the lead team, kept looking back impatiently now, talking with Ray Shields who was mounted on a free horse and who would be outrider.

When Frank had finished harnessing the team he had borrowed from the McGarritys, he looped up their tugs and tied them to the endgate of the buckboard.

Mounting his own horse now, he glanced down at the handful of the Saber crew which had been helping. Jess Irby's expression was one of skepticism; he shook his head and saw Frank watching him. "That's five thousand dollars on one rope, Frank; take care of it."

It was an hour short of noon when Frank rode past Johnny and said briefly, "Get 'em movin'."

By the time the long string was out of the meadows headed toward Rifle, both Johnny and Red had learned to keep the tugs tight, and Frank relaxed a little. His gamble might succeed, although the success of it hinged on his beating Rhino's bunch to Crawford; and they were some seventeen hours ahead of him. The advantage, however, lay with him, for Rhino's crew did not know they were in a race, and they would loiter, grazing their horses at every opportunity.

Two miles short of the grade into Rifle at the turnoff to O-Bar, Frank reined up and waited for the string. Once they caught up with him, he untied the McGarritys' team, and gave directions for skirting town so as not to arouse Rhino's curiosity. They were to pick up the river road below town, through O-Bar's range, and keep traveling until an hour after dark.

He watched them go, afterward hazing the loose team ahead of him down the road, and he was presently above town. It was not until he was off the grade and on the edge of Rifle that he really made up his mind to see Carrie. To explain to her that his plan was conceived in anger and planned in defiance and was to be carried out with some risk would only baffle her, and he had no intention of telling her where he was going. She would ask why he wanted to antagonize Rhino, and where was there an answer to that? Nevertheless, he wanted to see her.

He hazed his two horses into the side street, and presently approached Tavister's house, dark and cool in its lawn under the big trees.

The two loose horses, seing the lush grass of the Tavisters' lawn between the brickwall and the road, moved over and started to graze it.

Frank, some distance behind them, saw Carrie kneeling along a bed of flowers in front of the house, pointing out something to their handyman beside her. When she saw the horses stop, she rose and ran swiftly to the iron fence.

"Get away!" she scolded. "You get away!"

Frank reined up in the road and grinned. Carrie saw him and called, "Can't you keep—" and then, recognizing him, left the rest unspoken. Frank rode up now and Carrie cried in exasperation, "Frank, they're tramping our lawn!"

"Boys, quit it," Frank said mildly to the horses. They went on grazing, and now Carrie had to laugh. Frank stepped out of the saddle and moved across the walk to the iron fence. Carrie looked cool and small, and her face was alive and still lovely from her laughter.

"Shall I ask them in?" she asked.

"No, they're shy," Frank said solemnly.

Carrie raised up on tiptoe to kiss him, and then she folded her arms along the top of the fence's blunt-end iron pickets.

She said, "Stay for supper?"

"I'm horse-trading," Frank said. "I'll be gone for a few days."

"Not through Saturday," Carrie protested. "Oh, Frank, there's a dance Saturday night at the Masonic Hall."

Frank thought a moment. "I don't think I'll be back."

Carrie accepted this with a sigh of resignation. "Who're you trading for? Rhino?"

"For Chess and Company, horse-traders."

"Who's the company?"

"The five thousand dollars I hope to clean up on the deal."

Carrie didn't smile. She said, "So you're not a rancher any more, but a horse-trader?"

"If all you've got to trade is horses, you're a horse-trader, aren't you?"

"Yes—if it's all you've got to trade."

Frank grinned swiftly. "We aren't getting anywhere, are we?"

Carrie shook her head too, and then cradled her chin in her

67

arms and gazed across the street into the somnolent afternoon. "No, we aren't." She looked obliquely up at him. "Nice to be on the move again?"

Frank said, "Yes, we're in a hurry and—"he paused, looking down at Carrie. "You devil," he said mildly.

Carrie reached out and patted his hand. "That's all right. When you can't sit still, you can't sit still."

"That's not it," Frank protested. "I've got to make this trip, Carrie."

"So your feet will stop itching?"

Frank said in mock solemnity, "Some day, I won't come back."

"I believe you," Carrie answered soberly. And then, as if this conversation had taken too serious a turn, she straightened and made a shooing gesture with her hands. "Go on, go on. I've got flowers to water."

Frank moved over to his horse and mounted. Carrie wiggled her fingers at him and then called, "Please try to be back for the dance, Frank."

"I'll try," he promised, and now he whistled shrilly at the grazing team. They moved reluctantly back into the road, and he turned them at the next corner, driving them toward the main street. A vaguely guilty feeling remained with him now, when he thought of the dance. Carrie would like it, and he had been home so little lately that he had taken her nowhere.

He pushed his team across the main street, left them at the McGarritys' in care of a hostler, because neither Jonas nor John was in, and then he kept on to the river road and turned down-river. Presently, below town, he was on the main wagon road.

The horse string was somewhere ahead of him, he knew, but he was in no hurry to catch them. The heat here in the river bottom was a close and constant thing, held by the tawny rock of the gorge that sometimes crowded close to the river, only to fall back at other times for lush meadows and stands of river timber.

The memory of his parting with Carrie was a small and nagging worry in his mind now, taking the pleasure from the day. There had been an edge to her words today, as if the thought of his giving up Saber still rankled. And she had been quick and sly enough to make his few days' absence seem like his old restlessness, and his horse-dealing an obstinate whim. Perhaps her skepticism was justified, and now he examined his own feelings. It was true that he was glad to be on the move, to be away from Saber and town, and the reasons were plain enough. He wanted to avoid Hannan and his questions, and Rhino and his ultimatum. The flaw in that reasoning came to him immediately; he wasn't avoiding Rhino's ultimatum; he was merely postponing having to think about it.

He had reacted to that ultimatum promptly and recklessly, the way he had reacted to most things in his life, he understood now. He wanted to hurt Rhino, and getting his horses to Crawford ahead of Rhino's was a way to hurt him. Beyond that, he had reckoned it would give him a start and a stake—a start that would be stillborn and a stake that would be meaningless in the face of Rhino's threat.

That fact, Rhino's ultimatum, he had not faced. Looking at it closely now, he saw no way to avoid accepting Rhino as partner, for Rhino had summed it up precisely: *I can do anything I want with you as long as you're afraid of that soldier suit.* That was true; he could do anything. He had killed Rob and stopped Frank's mouth. He would get half of Saber, too. A bleak awareness of what this meant came to Frank then, and he thought, *He won't stop there; he wants it all.*

Almost under his horse's feet now, a quail with her four chicks broke out of the wayside brush and started across the road. The deep dust muffled the hoofbeats of the oncoming horse for a few seconds, and then the quail saw him and gave the alarm. She ran across the road, two chicks following her. The two chicks trailing, however, hesitated and dived back into the brush. Passing them, Frank saw them huddled in the brush, utterly still, their topnots unmoving. The sight of them scarcely stirred the moroseness of his thoughts.

In the late afternoon, he came to a wide meadow crossed by the road, with a thick fringe of trees back against the tawny canyon wall. There was track of a wagon, hours old, across the meadow and Frank glanced over at the fringing trees. Under them he saw a loaded wagon, apparently abandoned.

Kneeing his horse off the road he cut across the meadow, and when he rode up to the wagon he saw it was a big, high-sided freight wagon stacked high with a clutter of household furnishings. Off through the trees in the deep shade were four horses, heads to rumps, stomping flies.

And then, from under the wagon, he heard a puzzling sound, and he dismounted and looked. Stretched out in deep sleep was a man he recognized as Bill Schulte, one of Rhino's teamsters. A stone jug sat upright at his head.

Frank retrieved the jug and shook it, and it seemed half-full. He regarded Schulte idly; this was the breed of teamster that Rhino was going to lick the McGarritys with.

He uncorked the jug and took a long pull at the raw whiskey, then swung the jug against a wheel hub. It shattered heavily; Bill Schulte did not stir in his drunken sleep.

Frank mounted and sought the road again, the whiskey warming him pleasantly. Schulte, he remembered, was one of Tess Falette's charges, and he found himself recalling her story of yesterday with an odd pleasure now. He remembered how troubled she seemed when she told it. Oddly, there was something friendly and easy and unworried about her, and he found himself smiling at the thought of Carrie firmly trying to make over her life, and of Tess just as firmly refusing to have it made, and of how unlike they were.

But when the warmth of the whiskey wore off, his old mood returned, and it deepened with darkness, its torment deepening, too, so that an hour after dark, when he came to a large meadow and saw the flicker of his crew's campfire reflected high up on the canyon walls, he thought it a welcome sight.

He skirted the center of the meadow where the horses were grazing, and dismounted short of the fire. Three of the crew were in their blankets, already sleeping. He off-saddled, and Cass rode in out of the night to pick up his horse. Cass hazed the sorrel toward the bunch and then he reined up.

"I'm calling Johnny at midnight. There's grub on the fire, and your blankets are under the trees."

Frank thanked him and tramped toward the fire. He was not hungry, and a grinding weariness was on him.

Pulling off his boots then, he rolled into his blankets and lay there, staring at the tangle of low stars overhead, his depression deep and black as the night above him.

The futility of his being here tonight, of even starting this, came to him with a sickening stealth, and he tried again to find some small reason in what he was doing. There was none save that it would hurt Rhino, and Rhino, with Saber coming to him, could afford that hurt.

Chapter 10

THERE WAS A NOT-TOO-STRICT ROUTINE which Hugh Nunnally followed every morning after the lot opened up. He liked to leave the restaurant after an early breakfast, with a fresh cigar lighted, and saunter down the side street past McGarritys' to the river, just as the town was coming awake. This route eventually brought him to the rear of Rhino's lot, and each morning he paused by the gate in the rear fence and looked at the tracks in the dirt. The hostlers had strict orders to take every horse on the lot down to the river once a day to drink, since they kept better if this were done than if they were watered from buckets or a tank. It was an onerous job, and the hostlers shirked it, but Hugh, from long practice, could read in the tracks whether or not his orders had been carried out fully, half-carried out, or skipped entirely.

Today, with the forty-odd horses cleared out for Crawford and no new stuff come in, the sign was easy to read. All the horses had been driven to water. He strolled through the back gate and headed for the big stable, in a corner of which the sick and ailing horses were stabled. He always had a look at them, afterward glancing at the big manure pile to see if the corrals and stables had been cleaned.

By this time the crew would be gathered at the big stable, and he would assign them work. Then, moving up toward the office, he would stop at the barns and have a look at any new grain or hay that had been brought in while he was absent. He kept a careful check on the quality of feed, and he was strict about it. Somewhere along here in the process, he would remem-

71

ber Tess and send a man to the office to learn her freighting needs. Once he knew them, he would pick the teams, choose teamsters, name the wagons, and then move on toward the office.

This morning, after he had greeted her, he paused just outside the railing. "The McGarritys are beginnin' to board up."

"Are they? I hadn't noticed," Tess said pleasantly.

Hugh started to move on, then paused, and said, "I couldn't be lucky enough to have you say nobody's asked to take you to the dance Saturday, could I?"

Tess smiled. "No. I'm already asked."

Hugh gave her a friendly grin and moved on down the corridor to Rhino's office. Rhino was seated in his swivel chair, his feet on the window sill beside his desk. He and Hugh greeted each other pleasantly, and Hugh sat down, saying anew, "The McGarritys are beginning to board up."

"Damn bullheads," Rhino growled.

"Virg Moore got in last night," Hugh observed. "I sent him out to Ed Hanley's for a couple of days."

Rhino smiled, but said nothing, and they were both quiet a moment. Then Rhino said, "Any talk around town about our ruckus with Frank?"

"No," Hugh said. "Willie Haver don't even know what happened. Hannan's quiet about it."

"Tavister wouldn't have heard?"

"No," Hugh said. "That's my guess, anyway."

Rhino hoisted himself to his feet and stretched enormously. There was a faint twinkle in his bleak eyes now as he observed, "Time to work on him, then." He picked up his battered Stetson from the desk and moved ponderously out of the office and outside.

It was another bright day, and the sun felt good in his face, so he took off his hat and carried it. Passing the few mean shacks that lay between the lot and the business part of town, he spoke pleasantly to a raggedly dressed little girl behind a sagging fence. She answered hesitantly, her manner puzzled, as if she were wondering what this benevolent-looking Santa Claus was doing without his beard.

At the four-corners, he stopped for a chat with Mrs. Maas, and then cut across the street to the bank corner and mounted the stairs alongside the bank.

Judge Tavister looked up from a book at Rhino's courteous tap on the frame of the open door.

"Busy, Judge?"

At Judge Tavister's spare smile of welcome, Rhino came ponderously in, and they shook hands.

"I don't often see you, Rhino," Judge Tavister observed.

"Well, a horse-dealer always tries to stay away from a judge," Rhino remarked, and Judge Tavister smiled again. Rhino knew he could afford to make this joke, and he also knew Judge Tavister knew it too, which put them on an amiable footing. Judge Tavister indicated a chair, which Rhino settled into gently.

"I see your daughter around more than I do you, Judge," Rhino observed.

"She works. I loaf."

Rhino chuckled. "Well, now that Frank's back for good, I suppose she hasn't much time for her father."

The Judge gave Rhino another of his spare, non-committal smiles, and Rhino observed, in a suitably solemn voice, "I'm sorry he had to come home to Rob's death, though."

"That was unfortunate," Judge Tavister agreed.

Rhino frowned, and then asked in a polite but confidential manner, "Does Frank seem moody to you, Judge?"

Judge Tavister studied his desk a moment and then remarked dryly, "Yes, I can't quite blame him, though, considering the track Hannan has taken."

"A damned blunder," Rhino growled. "Hannan's a fool, and a clumsy one to boot. He's been annoying me, too, since Frank worked for me."

"Just what is he after? Hannan, I mean."

"Frank can't account for his whereabouts five days in July. Hannan seems to think Rob was killed then." Rhino snorted vastly. "I've had to send out for the man Frank was with to prove where he was."

"Let's hope your man has a better memory than Frank," Judge Tavister remarked. Rhino, upon reflection, thought that statement rather odd. It was time, however, for business, and now he asked, "Judge, you're handling Frank's affairs, aren't you?"

"I'm Rob's executor, if that's what you mean."

Rhino nodded. "Just how serious is Frank about wanting a partner?"

There was a five-second silence, while Judge Tavister regarded him closely. "A partner," the Judge said in a musing voice. "I didn't know he wanted one."

Rhino's thick black eyebrows raised slowly, slowly settled. "Then maybe I'm speaking out of turn."

The Judge said dryly, "Out of turn or not, I wish you'd speak. As his lawyer, I'd say I was privileged."

"All right. He came down to the lot the other night, talked with the boys awhile, and then drifted into my office. We talked about a lot of things, and finally Frank asked me how I'd like to go in partnership with him. Just like that."

"What did you tell him?"

Rhino spread his big hands expressively. "Why, I didn't know just what to say. I know what I think, though. I'm a horse-dealer working out of a two-by-four lot. If I hold a horse for two weeks, he's eaten up my profit. With a place to hold horses and grass to feed them, I could make money. And that's what Frank offered."

"Saber, you mean."

"Yes, I was to supply the cash. Frank would buy horses and supply the graze. I'd sell them." Rhino smiled almost wistfully. "For a horse-dealer, that's heaven."

Judge Tavister looked at a pigeonhole in his desk for a full minute, then he asked, "What's worrying you, Rhino?"

"Is he serious?"

"If he is, it'll be the first time he ever has been," Judge Tavister said tartly. He glanced at Rhino then and smiled apologetically. "I'm hard on him, perhaps. Still, just to give you a sample of what I'm up against with him, the last thing he said to me was to put Saber away for him. He didn't want it."

Rhino shook his big head wonderingly, and was silent.

Judge Tavister closed his eyes and rubbed them with thumb and forefinger of his thin hand, and then he made a wry grimace and shook his head sharply. "He's not steady."

"He worked well for me," Rhino said stoutly. "He's the sharpest horse-buyer I know."

Judge Tavister shrugged. "Maybe you can handle him."

"He doesn't need handling."

"I didn't mean that, exactly. I meant, maybe you're the partner for him."

That was what Rhino was waiting to hear, but he only looked
pleasantly baffled.

Judge Tavister said thoughtfully, "You've got a good thing
in that horse lot, haven't you, Rhino?"

This was no time for mock modesty, Rhino knew; he nodded
and said, "Have had, for twenty years."

Judge Tavister stood up now, and Rhino rose too. "I'll talk
with Frank," the Judge said.

They shook hands and Rhino went out. On the stairs he
paused to light up a cigar, and he was smiling gently. The news
that Frank was taking a partner, when it came, would be no
surprise now. The Judge even thought he would be a steadying
influence on Frank, Rhino struck a match and held it to his
cigar, but the irony of this last was so perfect that he began to
chuckle softly, and the chuckle blew out the match.

Chapter 11

BELLIED DOWN in the loose caprock which still held the heat
of the desert day, Frank regarded the activity below him, and
he did not like what he saw. Rhino's crew had chosen this
meager meadow astride the road in the angle of a shallow dog-
leg canyon for their last camp before Crawford, and the first
smoke of their fire was lifting into the deepening dusk of the
canyon. Frank noted that Pete Faraday had made camp at the
lower end of the meadow close to the wagon road, where the
canyon walls crowded close together. Fort Crawford lay only
twenty-odd miles to the south on the Ute Reservation, and there
was enough Indian in Pete to recognize that his loose band of
forty-odd horses, however well guarded, was a tempting prize
for any prowling Ute. Accordingly, he had blocked the exit to
the canyon in the best way he could—which put him almost

astride the road over which Frank's string must be driven to-night.

In the lowering dusk, Frank tried to identify at this distance the two men with Pete, and he recognized only Albie Beecham, a slight and wiry puncher so wickedly truculent that Rhino kept him away from towns as much as possible. The other man who, from horseback, was now passively watching the horses roll in the sparse grass, he did not know.

Frank watched a few minutes longer, and pulled back from the caprock until the rim was between him and the camp, and then he rose and started back toward his horse ground-haltered a hundred yards back on a sage thicket. If he was to beat Rhino's bunch to Crawford, the choice was plain enough; he could boldly drive his string past Pete's camp tonight, trusting to the hour and the darkness to hide the brands and the identity of his crew. That was leaving much to chance, though, for Pete Faraday would be wary. For while Rhino was always favored by the Fort Crawford quartermaster, Lieutenant Ehret, with in-formation about when mounts would be required, there was no assurance that other horse-dealers had not procured the same information. And Pete Faraday, seeing forty horses pass him in the night headed for Crawford, might logically think another dealer was pushing in ahead of him, and there would be trouble. The other choice, of course, was to break through.

Frank found his horse and mounted and turned back along the flinty, sunblasted road, already knowing what would have to be done. This desert canyon country along the edge of the Gunnison Gorge a mile to the west was laced by steep-walled, boulder-strewn washes, and there was no other way through it. An anger almost pleasant stirred in Frank now. For two nights and two days he had pushed his string ceaselessly down out of the mountains, away from the Grand River, and into the desert, using every hour of daylight and crowding every mile he could into the day's drive, and increasingly the uselessness of his errand had been brought home to him. Only a cross-grained obstinacy, sweat into him by this desert, had prevented him from turning back, since in another week none of this would matter anyhow. And now this whim of Pete Faraday's in placing his camp had brought the crisis, and grimly, Frank welcomed it.

It was full dark when he came to the wide wash slanting

down to the Gunnison where the string was lined out against a cutbank, indistinct in the darkness. In midafternoon, Frank had stopped the string here, and while the sweating crew took the horses down to water in the Gunnison, let them roll in the warm sand, and grained them, he had patiently observed Rhino's crew and waited for them to camp. Following his instructions, his crew had made no fire, and now the string, halted and harnessed again, was ready to travel. Cass, Red, Johnny, and Ray Shields were sprawled out on the bank, the coals of their cigarettes a dim beacon to him as he rode up and dismounted.

Briefly, then, he described the canyon and the location of Faraday's camp, and as he talked he wished there were a fire so he could see the faces of these men. There was nothing in their bargain that called for this, and the chill inference in his words would not escape them. They were silent when he finished, and it was Johnny Samuels who spoke first.

"You figure to sneak by 'em, Frank?"

Cass snorted around his pipe. "You been listenin' to forty horses for two days, Johnny. You think they wouldn't wake you up?" Cass's voice was rough and husky; as the wheel rider, he had been in a constant pall of dust for two days now, and his throat was raw.

It remained for Red Thornton to sum it up. "Hell, we got to ram through."

Frank remained out of the discussion until Ray Shields spoke, and then he knew they had accepted this as necessary. He tramped back to the buckboard, and brought out the lantern and lighted it, and afterward they squatted around it and planned their moves, Frank drawing a rough map in the dirt to guide them. There was no use trying to make an approach by stealth, they agreed. Better to hang the lantern on the collar of Johnny's lead horse, so that, rounding the dog-leg in the canyon, their coming would be announced plainly. Frank and Ray Shields, under cover of the racket kicked up by the string, would follow them, but at the dog-leg they would drift out into the meadow under cover of darkness. There would be a night-herder guarding Rhino's horses, of course, and both he and his horses would be alerted by the lantern. Once the dog-leg had been rounded, the string would be halted until Frank and Ray were above the herd. Then they would stampede Rhino's horses toward the camp and the canyon exit. The string would pull in at the tail end of the stampede at a dead run, trusting to the confusion to break through. Frank and Ray would swing in behind them, keeping Rhino's crew away from the string. If the stampede were effective, Pete Faraday would spend at least tomorrow beating the hot canyons running to the Gunnison, for his horses.

Frank borrowed Cass's gun and shell belt, for Hannan still had his, and while Cass and Red and Johnny mounted, he hung the lantern on the lead ring.

The string pulled out of the wash, past him, onto the road, and afterward he mounted, falling in beside Ray tailing the buckboard. There was, he knew, the chance of failure in this plan. If things went wrong, he was risking injury to his string and a wicked fight with an angry, hard-case crew. Once he recognized that, he settled into forced patience. His lips were dry and cracked, and he felt a grinding, burnt-out weariness as he pulled up his neckerchief over the lower half of his face against the dust.

Later, when the slope into the canyon began, and the teams lifted into a trot so that Cass had to brake the buckboard with his rope, he knew there was no turning back now. He peered ahead past the distant lantern, trying to see through the dust. The deep black was unbroken.

The road began to level out now and Frank knew the dog-leg was almost here. He leaned out and touched Ray Shields' arms, and then spurred his horse, moving up past Cass, Ray behind him.

Now Johnny, holding the lead team wide, swung around the turn of the dog-leg, and the lantern was gone from sight. Red began to curse, holding his team to the outside of the curve, too, reining back to keep the line taut. Over the backs of the teams as they took the turn, now, Frank saw the flickering campfire at the far end of the canyon, and now he put his attention on the meadow. He moved out toward it, keeping to the canyon wall on the left and its black shadows. He and Ray rode slowly, and as his eyes became accustomed to the darkness, he made out Rhino's horses standing, motionless, probably watching the distant lantern.

Then the form of the night-herder, his horse pointed toward

the lantern, was silhouetted against the far fire. Frank glanced to his right and saw the string's lantern cease movement, and in the same moment the night-herder moved his horse slowly toward it.

Frank knew then that this was the time to move, that the night-herder must get no nearer the string.

He pulled back and around, giving Ray's horse a slap across the rump with his hat as he passed, and then, heading directly for the herd of horses, he lifted his horse into a run, pulled his gun and mouthed a wild rebel yell. His shot and Ray's came almost together, and Ray let out a piercing whistle that cut the night like a knife.

Rhino's nearest horses, already made uneasy by the mysterious light on the road, panicked away from the sudden shouts and shots and yells, and it was only a matter of seconds before the fright of the few was communicated to the many. There was only one way they could run, and that was away from the noise and toward the fire, and as they grouped together for company, Frank could hear the mounting rumble of their hooves hammering the rocky ground as they fled. Glancing over to the string, now, he saw the lantern arc out into the night and snuff out, and he knew that Johnny had doused it before the string started to move again.

Behind him and to the side now he heard a wild cursing. The night-herder, caught between two choices, had waited too late to quiet the horses and they were away from him. Now he shot, and Frank saw in the man's hesitation that he had read this aright. He was heading for the string, shooting at it.

Frank swerved his horse sharply, riding now to head off the night-herder, who was angling across the meadow toward the string, invisible now in the night. His course, Frank saw, would converge soon with his own, and he held his fire, knowing his own location was undetected.

He stole a glance over his shoulder now, and saw that the two men at the fire had not mounted, and he knew their horses had been turned out with the bunch and they were afoot. They were standing in front of the fire now, waving blankets, trying to turn the oncoming stampede, and then he saw them dive for the shelter of the canyon wall as the wave of rampaging, terror-filled horses hit the camp. He saw the fire killed in an explosion

79

of sparks, and then he turned his head to pick up the night-rider.

At that very instant he was aware that he had overshot. He heard the night-rider's horse upon him and then something slammed into his sorrel with the force of an avalanche. He felt his horse falling, and he kicked free of the stirrups before he was hurled into the air. He landed heavily on his shoulder, while to the side of him he heard his horse crash to the ground. And mingled with this was the sound of a mighty weight falling on his horse, driving the breath from him in a great growling, grunting squeal.

Frantically, then, knowing the second horse had piled onto his sorrel, he drove his boots into the gravel, pushing himself away from the tangle. The night-rider's horse seemed in that darkness to do a complete somersault over the sorrel, and he hit the ground with an earth-stirring impact only feet away from Frank's head. Frank heard a bone snap, heard the squeal of terror, and he rolled wildly away from the thrashing animal. And with this cold urgency driving him, he heard the hoarse idiotic shouting of Cass in the dim distance, hazing the string into the canyon.

He lay there only seconds, his shoulder numb, his breath coming in great gasping heaves and the sound of it drowned by the noise of the thrashing animal. When he heard a horse floundering to its feet a moment later, only then did he realize that he was afoot, and that he must catch his horse or fight his way out. Where was the night-herder?

He stumbled to his feet, fell, and heard the horse walking in the night to his right. He rose and ran toward the sound, and then, despairingly, he heard the horse bolt, settle into a trot, and finally into a gallop. He could make out the shadowy form of the brute running for the canyon mouth and the other horses.

And then, yards behind him, he heard Albie Beecham's voice, wild and high-pitched in anger, calling, "Here's a man down! Here's one down, Pete! Build up the fire!"

Chapter 12

FRANK KNELT and lay down then, utterly still, realizing only now that his hand, as numb as his right arm and shoulder, still held his gun. *They'll hunt me down*, he thought narrowly, accepting this as the price he knew he might have to pay. It was not important now that the string had got through and vanished: this was real and immediate.

Behind him in the darkness he could hear the continued thrashing of the crippled horse, and he knew he must use the cover of this noise to move to safety. He rose and ran toward the road and the canyon wall. Suddenly, the night stillness was shattered by a single shot, coming from somewhere behind him. Albie had shot the horse so he could hear him, he knew, and now he was acutely aware of the cold and wicked threat of this.

Even now, the man at the camp fifty yards ahead of him was kicking at the coals of the fire, fanning them with his hat into a small blaze. By its meager light he could see the watchful shape of Pete Faraday prowling the middle of the road, blocking the canyon exit. He knew that Albie Beecham behind him would have only to wait for more fire, then move slowly toward any near sound in the night, and he would have him silhouetted against the far blaze. Then a careful shot would do it.

Go back? No, the threat was still there, and his friends were ahead. Try and ram through? Not with Pete ahead of him. With Albie behind him, and the third man at the side, he would have no chance he knew. If he moved across the meadow to the east, Albie was sure to pick up his silhouette. Only one route of escape lay open, and that was the canyon wall beyond the road some thirty yards away. He tried to remember the slope of the wall, and could not, although he recalled it was only thirty or forty feet high. Thinking of this now, he did not like it, but the urgency to get out of here was on him and he did not hesitate. He moved cautiously toward the road, bending far over to use the low screening brush for a shield, straining his

81

hearing for the slightest sound indicating that Albie had picked him up.

Pete Faraday yelled now, "Sing out, Albie!" but Albie was quiet, unwilling to give his position away. The fire was slow in catching: even when built up, Frank guessed, its light would not reach here.

He moved more swiftly now, the low brush giving him some shelter, and then he was across the road and against the cliff. He straightened slowly, feeling the texture of its surface. It was live rock, and would not crumble under his weight.

Ramming his gun in his belt, he found a toe-hold and began to climb out of this trap. He had gone a silent and laborious ten feet when he felt his back tighten at a sound below him. Albie, emboldened, was cruising around now. Frank listened, feeling the skin in his back crawling, shrinking.

Then Albie called sharply, "Pete, get up on the rim! He's between us!"

Frank watched narrowly while the man at the fire moved over to cover the road, while Pete vanished among the rocks at the canyon exit.

With infinite caution now, Frank felt for a handhold and moved up. The first gentle slope of the canyon wall was straightening now toward the perpendicular, and he was sweating with the urgency and effort of silence. Surely, if Albie raised his eyes, he must see him. Below and back toward the dog-leg, he heard Albie's swift and hungry prowling.

He concentrated desperately now, moving with infinite caution. Above him he felt for a handhold, and his fingers slipped into a deep crevice, dislodging a pebble. He stiffened, feeling the pebble tumble, and he listened while it fell, hitting the wall twice, and sharply, before it spattered into the gravel at the bottom.

Albie caught the sound. He yelled shrilly, "Hurry, Pete!" but he did not move, and Frank knew then that Albie could not see the canyon wall in the darkness.

He worked desperately then; looking above him he saw the black rimrock silhouetted against the stars. And now agonizingly he could find no handhold, and he wasted precious minutes moving along the crevice where he had his foothold, until his hands encountered a crack that would give him a purchase.

He pulled himself up, and heard Albie cursing softly, impatiently somewhere below him. The rimrock was close now. He kept watching it, working toward it, and when he reached it he pulled himself up until his head was almost even with it. Pausing, he wiped the sweat from his hands, and sought a fresh toe-hold to his right now. He swung up, and his chest was against the smooth rock of the rim.

Remembering that he would be silhouetted now, he paused stilling his breathing, listening for Pete. There was no sound, and reassured, his muscles were tensed for the final heave up when a faint sound reached his ears. It was a brushing, whispering sound that was there only a moment, and then was not. He lay motionless, listening, trying to identify the sound. And then it came to him. *That damn Indian has taken off his boots.*

Frank's hand traveled to his gun now. He pulled it noiselessly, held it muffled against his shirt as he pulled back the hammer and stretched his arm out on the rock in front of him, the gun cocked. From his low vantage-point against the rimrock, anything moving along the canyon's edge was silhouetted against the stars.

He waited, breath held, hearing Albie's bitter cursing below, listening beyond this distraction. And then a vague form took shape in the night, moving with the slow stealth of a hunting animal. Closer now, it took the form of a man, and he was keeping back from the rim. Frank stilled his breathing. If the whisper of Pete Faraday's sock feet once paused, he must shoot.

Peter moved closer now, and like a wraith drifted in front of him, in front of his gun, and passed on. Some ten feet beyond Frank, he changed his course, feeling with sure feet for the edge of the rimrock. He was going to have his look over the edge.

He halted, and now, almost hesitantly, his suspicions aroused by something, he began to move back toward Frank. Frank moved his arm to cover him, and his shirt whispered almost inaudibly against the rock as his arm moved.

Pete caught the sound: his movement was swift then. Frank sensed it, and swung his gun around and fired immediately. He heard the slug hit, heard Pete grunt, and saw him jerk around, and then there was a raking sound against the rock, followed by three full seconds of silence before the heavy, soft thud

83

below him told him Pete had fallen. He scrambled over the rimrock now, careless of the noise he made, as he heard Albie calling wildly, "Pete, Pete! Who's hit?"

Afterward, Albie shot, but it was only temper, and he was shooting at nothing. Frank lay on his belly, pressing his cheek against the warm rock, and he was shaking and angry at himself for it. When he heard a man running below, he raised his head and saw that the man at the fire, attracted by Albie's shot, was joining him in the meadow.

He should move, he knew, but he lay there a moment longer before he rolled over, pulled off his boots, and rose. Moving back from the rim now, he traveled at a steady pace to the south, until he had placed the fire far behind him.

The next fifteen minutes he spent finding a way down the canyon wall, and when he was presently on the road in the canyon's cleft, he halted. There was little danger of being followed, for both Albie and the other man were afoot. Frank wondered now whose downed horse had been silenced by Albie's shot, his own or Albie's. If it was his sorrel, then the evidence was there for Rhino to read. Whosoever it was, he didn't care. Rhino had a man hurt or dead, his horses scattered, his crew afoot, and, unless something had happened to the string, Rhino stood to lose a five thousand dollars sale of horses. Frank felt a deep and wicked satisfaction in that as he turned down the narrow canyon road.

It was some minutes before he picked up the sound of a horse being carefully ridden toward him. He drifted back against the canyon wall, and when the rider finally was abreast of him he called softly, "Ray?"

"Who is it?" Ray Shields' voice was wary and hard.

"Me. Frank."

Frank walked over to him and he heard Ray swearing softly in relief.

"I never even saw you after we started, Frank. What happened?"

Frank told him, and afterward asked, "Did the string get through?"

"They ran for four miles before they could be stopped. No horses hurt, nobody hurt. They weren't even shot at." Ray laughed with relief. "Rhino's bunch are strung along the Gunnison Canyon for five miles."

Frank said, "Did you run across a loose horse down the road?"

"Albie's. I hid his saddle and choused the horse up a canyon." He hesitated. "That all right?"

It's all wrapped up for you, Rhino, Frank thought, and he answered quietly, "That's fine."

Chapter 13

FORT CRAWFORD was a new post, begun in early spring as a counterthreat to Ouray and his restive Utes who had declined to submit to reservation authority. Two troops of cavalry from Fort Garland, three hundred miles to the east, had been sent to construct and garrison the post, which lay on a dry triangle of sage flats between two creeks that funneled out from the beginning foothills of the Rockies' western slope.

Approaching it now from the north and the west, its few log buildings and its ranks of Sibley tents which still housed the troopers seemed lonely and insignificant against the vast backdrop of towering Black Mesa behind it. The flag drooped lifelessly in the blazing midday sun from its pole at the head of the parade ground, stirred only by an occasional scurrying dust devil blown in from the desert to break on the far foothills.

A few Ute lodges, their skins rolled up from the ground to catch any stray breeze, were clustered to the south, and Frank, who had delivered a bunch of Rhino's replacement mounts to the post in the spring, saw little change. The adobe corrals and stables to the east were finished, the drop logs of a few more buildings around the rectangular parade ground laid, and a few rows of logs added to the long barracks on the north side. Stacks of fresh-cut pine lumber from the mills in the mountains lay darkening in the sun. Riding ahead of the string now, Frank could hear a lackadaisical hammering, and there was already the air of deliberation and timelessness about the place that characterized all Army establishments.

A handful of troopers strolled out between the tents to watch the string pass on the way to the quartermaster corrals. Frank dropped back to chase off a pair of yapping Indian curs who were snapping at Johnny's leaders, and he glanced over the outfit. The crew was sun-blackened and dusty, their shirts ringed with the white salt stains of sweat, but the horses were in good shape.

He lifted his horse into a lope and went on ahead, turning past the north stable and heading for the big quartermaster corral. Lieutenant Ehret, he knew, would remember him, and since Rhino's horses were expected, the lieutenant would assume Frank was still working for Rhino. This might help in the inspection but Frank didn't really care; these horses were good, and he knew an honest vet or line officer could not turn up faults in any of them.

He dismounted by the big corral where a dusty blue-clad trooper was already opening the gate, and dispatched him for Lieutenant Ehret. Frank waved the string on into the vast corral, closed the gate, and then, leading his horse, he tramped over to the trough, where fresh water was running from a pipe. He drank deeply from the pipe, and then, while he waited for his horse to drink, he went back in his mind over the routine of the inspection. The trouble, of course, would come when the check for payment was made ou and Lieutenant Ehret was requested to make it out to him instead of Rhino. For Lieutenant Ehret, when allowed to use discretion in buying, had his favorites, and Rhino, wise in the ways of horse-dealing, had long since cemented his friendship with the quartermaster by presents and gifts. As a result whenever Lieutenant Ehret was directed to buy horses from the local market and not through requests for submission of bids, he sent a letter to Rhino stating his requirements and Rhino complied. By allowing other horse-dealers to remain in ignorance of those requirements, the whole thing was made easy and profitable to them both, and impeccably legal. When a little pressure was needed, that could be used too.

Frank remembered when another horse-dealer had tried to interfere, and this recalled a necessary chore. He left his horse and tramped across the corral to the fence separating the quartermaster corral from the north stable corral. There were twenty-odd horses in the small corral, most of them clustered in the shade of the stable roof's overhang. Frank only had to glance at them to identify the Starcross brand on three of them, and as he turned back he thought grimly, *I learned a lot of things from Rhino and Hugh.*

A half-dozen men in blue field uniform and black campaign hats came into the corral now, and Frank walked toward them. Lieutenant Ehret saw him coming and smiled, and stepped toward him, holding out a soft, white hand. He was a paunchy man, with a fold of belly overlapping his belt, and he had a ragged roan mustache, worn full, that covered a loose-lipped mouth.

He seemed tired and harried, but pleasant enough, and Frank guessed the post construction was largely his chore. He said, "How are you, son? How's friend Rhino?"

Frank told him, but already Lieutenant Ehret was looking at the string across the lot. They were still in line, for Frank wanted to keep them from water until the inspection was over. Frank shook hands with the contract veterinary, an old and mussed and amiable man in a careless uniform who remembered him from the spring and introduced him to the two young officers with him, Lieutenants Hardy and Relitch. Two troopers carrying saddles crossed over to the string.

Lieutenant Hardy was lean and young and ramrod-straight, just out of the Academy, and there was a kind of cheerful impudence latent in his face. He regarded the string a moment, then said, "How many are you buying, Ehret?"

"Forty, I asked for."

Hardy looked at Frank. "Not counting the buckboard team, you've got thirty-nine there."

Frank pointed to his own horse, which was still at the trough.

"Still that's only forty." Hardy grinned. "Don't you allow for rejections?"

"Not on this bunch," Frank said.

Hardy laughed and shook his head, and now they moved over to the string. Cass and Johnny had unharnessed the lead team, and now Cass led the first horse out in front of them. Lieutenant Ehret, already bored, sought the shade of the stable wall and sat down, while the vet and the two lieutenants looked over the horse for faults of conformation. Then the vet examined mouth and feet, and, finished, signaled one of the troopers to saddle the horse. Lieutenant Hardy mounted now, and Frank supposed he was substituting for Lieutenant Ehret as inspecting line officer. Hardy tried the horse for gentleness, and then galloped him to the far end of the corral and back, and reined up before the vet. This was the test for wind. The vet listened, and said, "Sound. Bring on the next."

Frank drifted over and squatted by Lieutenant Ehret in the shade, willing to let the horses show without help from him. Ehret observed pleasantly, "They're all the same brand, and they're a good bunch. Rhino ought to remember that brand."

Johnny Samuels overheard him, and he looked over his shoulder at Frank. Frank shook his head imperceptibly and said, "He will," with a faint irony that brought a glance but no comment from Ehret.

Only once was a horse questioned, and that was when Lieutenant Relitch suggested that a claybank gelding had a tendency to curby hocks. Lieutenant Hardy pounced on him, scoffing, and the vet backed up Lieutenant Hardy. Relitch rode the horse and was satisfied, and as the vet called for the next horse Relitch, glancing at Frank, said slyly, "Dammit, there must be something wrong with *one* of them."

Frank only smiled. When the forty horses finished inspection, Lieutenant Ehret heaved himself to his feet, and Frank rose too. Lieutenant Hardy came over, halted beside them, reached in his shirt pocket, and brought out a long black cigar, which he tendered to Frank.

"I don't owe you this," Hardy said, grinning, "but I made a bet with myself and lost."

Ehret laughed and clapped Frank on the shoulder. "I know my dealers," he said affably. "Come along for your money, son."

Frank shook hands with the two officers, and fell in beside Lieutenant Ehret, who seemed in great good humor. As they walked past the stables toward one of the few finished buildings on the parade ground, he explained the post construction, and Frank listened idly. They were chased off the drive by a big construction wagon filled with adobe, and afterward they entered a low, one-story log building bearing the sign Adjutant over the doorway. They were immediately in a big room holding several desks, behind which blue-clad troopers were working.

Lieutenant Ehret turned right, and paused before one of the desks, saying, "Make out a check for five thousand dollars, sergeant. Make it payable to J. J. Hulst, H-u-l-s-t, and bring it in for my signature."

Frank, from behind him, said mildy: "Better make that payable to me, Lieutenant Ehret. The name," he added to the sergeant, "is Frank Chess, C-h-e-s-s." He looked levelly at Ehret now. The startled look on Lieutenant Ehret's face was only momentary. He was about to speak, thought better of it, and said to the sergeant, "Hold on a minute, Grady." He led the way to one of the offices opening onto the room, stepped aside to let Frank enter, and then closed the door behind him.

His voice was still cordial, though wary, as he said now, "I hate to ask this, Chess, but have you any authority from Rhino for this? Some paper?"

"They're my horses," Frank said.

Ehret frowned, and let his hand fall from the doorknob. Frank, standing in the middle of the small office, watched the bafflement mount in Ehret's eyes.

"But these are Rhino's horses, aren't they?"

"No."

"You work for Rhino, though, don't you?"

"No."

"He sent you? Maybe he didn't have the horses at hand?"

"No."

Ehret said with a sudden suspicion, "How did you know I had called for horses?"

"Rhino said so."

Lieutenant Ehret looked searchingly at him and walked over to his desk, which was placed across the corner of the room, and sat down in the chair behind it. He said carefully, softly now, "What's going on here? I don't understand this."

"You wanted forty horses. You've got them, and they've passed inspection."

Ehret leaned back slowly in his chair. "I see," he said slowly. "You just beat Rhino to the post, is that it?"

Frank nodded. Ehret shook his head and said with a mild irony, "I think I'll wait for Rhino, Chess, if you don't mind."

"I do mind," Frank murmured. He walked over to Ehret's desk, put both hands on it, and said quietly, "You remember me, Lieutenant. I was here last spring with Nunnally delivering mounts. We got in after you and the vet had rejected sixty Starcross horses that Holborn over in Utah brought here. I was here with Nunnally when he bought the whole bunch from Holborn for forty dollars a head. I was here the next day, after Holborn left, when you bought that bunch and our bunch from Nunnally for a hundred and twenty-five dollars a head. Remember?"

Color crept into Lieutenant Ehret's face, and his eyes were ugly with dislike. Frank said now, "Those Starcross brands haven't been vented. Maybe the Major would like to see them out in the corral now."

He straightened up and waited, while Lieutenant Ehret's baleful glance rested on him.

"You young pup," Ehret said bitterly. "You wouldn't dare."

Frank turned on his heel and started for the door.

"Wait!" Ehret said sharply.

Frank halted and turned.

Ehret said, "I'll take ten of them."

"You'll take forty," Frank said, and he started for the door again.

"Hold on!" Ehret called sharply.

Again Frank paused and turned. Ehret was chewing the fringe of his mustache, glaring at Frank. "I'm acting absolutely within my orders in dealing with Hulst," he said flatly.

"Is it within your orders to reject sixty horses one day, and the next day, after they've changed ownership, accept them and pay a hundred and a quarter apiece for them?"

Ehret didn't answer.

"Let's ask the Major," Frank gibed.

Ehret sighed heavily and came to his feet. He crossed the room in front of Frank, flung open the door, and tramped over to the sergeant's desk. "Make out the check to this gentleman, Grady. Here, I'll sign it."

He signed his name to the blank check, and without a word or a look at Frank, he tramped past him back into his office and shut the door.

Frank pocketed the check and went out. In the bright sun, he stopped, folded the check and put it in his shirt pocket, feeling no elation, feeling nothing except a dismal resignation. He had used up all the rope, and he was at the end of it now. He was going back to take his medicine.

Chapter 14

T HE MASONIC HALL was on the four-corners above Carrington's General Store, and tonight wagons, buckboards, saddle horses and buggies overflowed the hitch-racks on the main street, and filled the side street. Teams were unhooked and tied to endgates where they could feed on the hay in the wagonbeds, for this would be an all-night dance. The whole country, from the Battle Meadows to the Grand Peaks, and all up and down the river, would come with box suppers and the children. The town closed up, save for the saloons, and by dark the fiddle and accordion music was pouring out into the main street through the open windows of the hall, for this was the only break in the long summer's work before round-up.

Through the open window of her room, Tess could hear the music, and she hummed along with the fiddles now as she stopped before the mirror, giving her pale hair a final caress. She wished the mirror were bigger, but she had no misgivings about her appearance. This was a foolish dress, all white with a low, tight-fitting bodice and short sleeves with gay blue ribbon threaded through them, but she liked it and it made her feel good each time she wore it.

She blew the lamp then and went down into the lobby, which was crowded with men in dark suits and couples waiting impatiently for other couples.

Jonas McGarrity broke away from a couple of scrubbed-looking punchers and met her at the foot of the stairs, a wondrous smile on his usually morose face. He wore a stiff black suit, and his burnished boots shone with the same splendor as his black, smooth hair. By the flush of his face and the brightness of his

91

eyes, Tess guessed he had made several trips to the Pleasant Hour. She was sure of it when he said with an unaccustomed gallantry, "I may not have a freighting outfit any more, Tess, but I've got the best-looking girl in town tonight."

"The McGarritys are Irish and the Irish flatter you," Tess said, laughing, but all the same she was pleased.

They crossed the street to the stairs leading up to the hall. A knot of shy punchers broke for them at the foot of the stairs. Tess dodged a half-dozen kids who were racing up and down the stairs in the last burst of the day's energy, and emerged into the big jam-packed hall. There was a quadrille being made up, and Tess had only the barest opportunity to look around the crowded room to wave to old Mrs. Bodine, and to hear Dick Afton, the O-Bar's foreman and the caller for tonight, announce the first set when Arch Ison, grinning his apologies to Jonas, swung her into the set that was formed.

The dance was breathless. The set was loaded with the men from the Horn Creek country, shirt-sleeved, weather-burned men who knew her from their own dances, and they whirled her and danced with the driving exuberance of friendly men who liked to tease. When the set ended, they gathered around her, and before Jonas could make his way to her the next dance started, and she was taken away again.

When this dance ended, Tess retreated into the women's coat-room and leaned against the wall to get her breath. The three women there smiled at her as they went out. Across the small room the table was loaded with the box suppers, and under the table in a big clothesbasket the Oberndorf twins were sleeping. Tess moved over and looked at them. She heard someone enter the room, and turned to look, her face still flushed with excitement of the dancing.

It was Carrie Tavister who had come in, and in one flickering second Tess saw the envy in her dark eyes, and she knew then, without pride, that Jonas had been right.

"I never see you, Tess," Carrie said in a cordial voice. "How beautiful you look."

Tess flushed, and she was exasperated with herself. She said, with a friendly smile, "You'd never think we lived in the same town, would you?"

Carrie nodded, and said with a quick grimace, "Sometimes I

wish that big barn of a house would burn down, so I wouldn't have to take care of it. It's a prison and I never get out of it."

She crossed over to the mirror on the wall. She was so short, Tess noticed, that she had to stand on tiptoe to see herself. Carrie pinched her cheeks to bring the color into them, and patted her shining black curls. She said then, with a sigh of self-derision, "If I saw this hair on a dog, I still wouldn't like it."

Tess laughed, and Carrie smiled too. There was a doll-like quality about Carrie that Tess recognized and appraised now; her dark green dress, rich-looking and undoubtedly expensive, molded her slight, full figure with a delicate and delicious skill. Only a faint sharpness in her eyes and a hint of a pinched look around the corners of her barely uptilted nose mirrored the deep discontent that Tess guessed was imprisoned within her. Oddly, she wondered if Frank could read this and was ever troubled by its presence. As for herself, she had made her peace with Carrie some two years back, and it still held in the form of an amicable truce. There was too much iron in this self-willed girl for Tess's tolerant way, and she guessed there was too much of the casual and easy acceptance of life in herself to suit Carrie's taste.

Tess said, "I haven't seen Frank tonight."

Carrie said dryly, "He's horse-trading somewhere," and came over to Tess now. She reached out to adjust the bow on Tess's sleeve, and now she asked idly, "What's it like to work for Mr. Hulst, Tess?"

"They're nice to me there," Tess said. "It's—oh, I guess it's better than teaching school. For me, anyway."

"Do you like Rhino?"

Tess said in a neutral voice what was the literal truth, "He's always been very pleasant to me."

"Does he make money? Is he a good businessman? I mean, that horse lot is so ramshackle and smelly there's no way of telling."

"I think his business is good. It's certainly big," Tess replied. This was an odd conversation, she thought, and she wondered what was behind it. Carrie must have understood her thoughts, for she smiled suddenly.

"I know it's silly, isn't it? Only, I've always wondered what sort of a man Rhino is, and if his old clothes and his shacky old place weren't a pose. I guess I've always accepted him since I was small, just like the scenery, but I've always been curious about him."

Tess nodded. "I know what you mean. For the same reason, some day I'm going into a barber shop and ask for a shave, just to see what it's like."

They both laughed then, and moved toward the door. Jonas was waiting outside to claim her, and Tess smiled good-bye to Carrie.

Jonas swung her into a varsoviana, and they hadn't danced long before Tess knew Jonas had been visiting the Pleasant Hour again. She accepted this with an easy tolerance because he seemed to be having a good time. When the dance ended, Jonas came to a halt that was not quite steady.

"Celebrating?" Tess asked.

Jonas grinned, but there was little humor in it. "That's right, Tess. I'm celebratin' goin' back to punchin' O-Bar cows again at thirty a month—just where I left off three years ago."

"That's only temporary, Jonas," Tess said comfortingly.

"Maybe," Jonas said with a sudden gloom. "Maybe it's as permanent as Rhino's bank account, too."

She was claimed by old Mr. Jackson for a schottische then, before she could comfort Jonas. After that, she danced with old friends she had not seen for months, and chatted with their womenfolk, and danced again and again. As the evening wore on, the children subsided; they sat big-eyed in the chairs along the wall, listening to tireless fiddles and Dick Afton getting more and more hoarse until they finally curled up and slept. She saw Judge Tavister dancing sedately with Mrs. Maas, and once, when she danced past crippled John Colby, the stage driver, he gave a grave nod of approval and winked.

It was a waltz that Hugh Nunnally finally claimed. His blocky, massive chest filled out his clean shirt solidly, and there was a kind of mocking courtliness about him that amused Tess. He danced expertly, offhandedly, the way he did everything, and he regarded her with the same bland good-humor he showed her every day. And, as always, she was faintly distrustful of that blandness, and of the unruffled confidence of the man that she had long since rightly read as an inner arrogance.

When the waltz was finished and he had just touched her

arm, she heard a voice from the other side of her say, "Evenin',
Tess, Hugh." She looked up to see Sheriff Hannan, affable and
smiling beside her. Hannan said to her, "You're looking beautiful this evening," and gave her an easy smile that she knew
was reserved for every woman in this room tonight.

Hannan glanced at Hugh then and said, "Virg Moore come
in from Utah today?"

"He ought to be in tonight, Buck," Hugh said. "I left word
for him."

Hannan nodded and drifted on, and now Tess said, "But
Virg Moore has been in from Utah for a couple of days, Hugh."

Nunnally smiled faintly and said, "I know. Hannan doesn't,
though. Don't worry your head about it."

In other words, she was to mind her own business, Tess
thought. When he delivered her back to a silent and hostile Jonas
and thanked her, it was with the same unruffled good-humor.

Dick Afton was forming a quadrille now, and she and Jonas
moved out into the center of the floor. She looked up then to
see Frank Chess standing in the doorway looking over the
crowd. He was in dusty work clothes, and there was a dark
smear of beard stubble on his face. He stood there, hands on
hips, hat held in one hand, his dark short hair curly and tousled,
and Tess saw the quick gay smile come to his face as he saw Carrie. Carrie made her way across the floor to him, hurrying, and
not caring who noticed it.

Jonas spotted Frank just as Carrie came up to him.

"There's Frank," Jonas said. He grabbed Tess's hand and
moved toward the door, pulling her behind him, calling "Frank,
come on and dance."

Frank glanced up and saw Jonas and smiled. His glance
shifted to Tess then, and Tess saw the quick approval that
mounted into his eyes. He said, "How are you, Tess?" in a
friendly voice.

Carrie was smiling happily beside him, and now Jonas said,
"Come on, Frank. These girls are dancing my legs down."

Frank shook his head and looked down at his clothes. "In
these clothes I couldn't get a partner, Jonas."

"You can't miss this," Jonas pleaded, and he glanced at
Carrie. "Tell him to get in here, Carrie."

Carrie looked up at Frank, and then touched his face with

95

her small hand, rubbing his beard stubble. She said, "Maybe they won't know him with the fur on."

Jonas said quickly, "Look, Frank. Come on over to my room. Shave and get on a clean shirt, and you'll be back in time for supper."

Tess watched Frank look down at Carrie inquiringly, and read her silent pleading, and then he glanced up and said, "All right, Jonas. It's on your head."

Jonas turned and called, "Arch," and Arch Ison tramped over. Jonas put Tess's hand in Arch's and then poked a long finger solemnly at Arch's chest. "This is a loan, understand?" He grinned at Tess and took Frank by the arm, and they went down the stairway.

Jonas stumbled once on the stairs and caught himself, and Frank, noticing it, looked sharply at him. He'd been drinking, Frank saw; a secret, alcoholic glumness sat strangely in Jonas's face and Frank wondered at it.

The McGarritys' rooms were over Miss Amy Dunn's dressmaking shop down the side street two doors behind the hotel, and access to them was by a rickety flight of wooden stairs along the side of the building.

Jonas preceded Frank through the doorway, turning left toward the front of the building. Frank waited inside until Jonas had struck a match and lighted the lamp, and then he came into the room. It was a small room, holding only an unmade bed littered with clothes, a couple of chairs, a stove in the far corner, and a washstand with mirror above it. These were poor man's quarters, and Jonas made no apology for them.

He said now, "You want to wait for hot water, Frank, or would you rather tear your face off?"

Frank rubbed his beard judiciously, and said he'd take cold water, and stripped out of his shirt. He poured the basin full of water and lathered his face and his upper body. He heard Jonas moving around behind him, then heard a glass set on the washstand, followed by the sound of bedsprings creaking. When he rinsed the soap from his eyes, he saw the glass with whiskey in it that Jonas had poured him, and he glanced at Jonas. He was sitting on the edge of the bed, the bottle between his feet, a drink in his hand, and a kind of brooding anger in his face now.

Frank said, "Where's John?"

"He took our horses to the mountain," Jonas said gloomily. He looked at his whiskey and said bitterly, "Startin' Monday, I'm back to punchin' cows again, Frank."

"Give Rhino time."

Jonas took a long swallow of his drink and shuddered. He said then, "You think Tess has this figured right? Rhino will quit when it begins to hurt?"

"I think mountain freighting in winter will break his heart," Frank said.

He began to lather his face, and Jonas rose and moved restlessly to the front window and looked out through it.

Frank glanced in the mirror, thinking soberly, *This is the fifth day.* He had stopped off at the dance, while the crew, weary and sleep-starved, went on through to Saber. It was only the memory of Carrie's disappointment that made him do it, and now he wondered if he had been wise. He had seen Hannan and Nunnally at the dance, and Nunnally had seen him, and tonight was Rhino's deadline. Some faint hope that this might be a bluff which must not remain uncalled prevented him from seeking out Rhino—that, and a deep reluctance to make the decision. He supposed Albie had returned with news of the stampede, or perhaps he was still scouting the canyons into the Gunnison for his scattered horses. There had been no sign of him on the way back from Crawford.

The first raw rake of Jonas's straight-edge razor hurt. He took a sip of the whiskey now, waiting for the soap to soften his beard. In the mirror he could see Jonas, still looking out the window into the night, and he noticed that Jonas was a little unsteady on his feet. On Tess's account he wondered how he could tell Jonas he'd had enough to drink for the night, but the thought trailed off as he remembered Tess and how exciting and beautiful she had seemed when he first saw her tonight. It was as if he were looking at her for the first time in her proper setting; she was all pale gold and white, softly proud and feminine, yet with the easy and friendly way about her that made all people want to like her. She was exciting and warm, and he found himself wondering if all men felt like this about her, and he knew they did.

The sound of Jonas turning away from the window now

broke into his reverie. He began to shave, and Jonas came back to the bed. "Every time I look out that window at the office, I get mad all over again," Jonas growled.

Before Frank could say anything, there was the sound of footsteps on the outside stairs. Jonas rose, just as the outside door opened. Hugh Nunnally came slowly in, Morg Lister and Virg Moore trailing him. Moore was a slight puncher, with a determined, oversized jaw that badly needed shaving, and which, in his case, reflected only the determination to drink more than he could hold. He was sober enough now, though, and he stank of horses. He smiled uneasily at Frank, as if he had been forbidden to, but couldn't find a way around it.

Nunnally put a shoulder against the wall and said unsmilingly, "Going to the dance, Frank?"

Jonas stepped out into the middle of the room and halted on unsteady legs. He raised a hand and pointed a finger at Nunnally, and said, in a voice thick with both whiskey and outrage, "I don't like you, and especially I don't like you in my room. You can take those other two dogs and get out."

Hugh regarded him a calm moment, then pushed away from the wall, took an easy step toward him, and hit him. It was a solid blow, swung with all the corded strength of Hugh's thick shoulder, and Jonas hadn't expected it. He went down against the bed, and his head rapped sharply against the bedframe. He lay there loosely, eyes closed.

Frank's weight was on his toes when he heard Lister say sharply from the doorway, "All right, Frank!"

He saw the gun pointed at him now, and he settled back on his heels, looking wrathfully at Nunnally.

"Frank's all right," Hugh said mildly. "Now lug McGarrity into the back room, you two."

Hugh moved back against the wall, and Lister and Moore picked up Jonas and carried him back into the other bedroom. Hugh watched Frank now with a level, hard aggressiveness in his eyes that canceled the pleasant half-smile on his straight mouth.

"Albie brought your saddle in," Hugh observed then, and he shook his head in wonderment. "The only trouble with you Frank, is that you killed Pete in front of the wrong witnesses."

"He tried for me."

Hugh said boredly, "I know. You can tell all that to a United States Marshal and a federal jury."

Moore and Lister came back now, but Frank did not look at them. He was watching Hugh, trying to reach for the meaning behind Hugh's words. Hugh saw his puzzlement and he smiled now. "You see, Rhino's got the letter from Lieutenant Ehret requesting the mounts. Pete was on Army business, you might say, when he was killed on reservation land. The Army can't let its contractors be terrorized." He shrugged. "Once Rhino complains, it's the Army's affair, and they'll work through a United States Marshal."

Frank looked down at the razor in his hand; he had forgotten it. He turned now and resumed his shaving, thinking over what Hugh had said, and he saw with a bitter clarity that Hugh was right. He did not even have to ask the price of Rhino's silence, for he already knew it. Like a fly caught in a web, the more he struggled the deeper he became enmeshed, and his small triumph over Rhino had been turned into yet another weapon against him.

He heard Hugh say to Moore and Lister, "Wait down on the street for me, will you?"

The two of them tramped outside and down the stairs. Frank went on shaving, knowing Hugh was watching him, knowing what was coming. He hadn't pictured it as happening like this; he had imagined a bitter argument, and a long process of bargaining before he acknowledged defeat. The possibility of that was gone, now, and at last he was solidly up against the choice. He thought of Carrie, the only decent thing in his life, and he knew now as he had known five days ago that he would do everything in this world to keep her.

Hugh said in a casual voice, "I'm taking Virg to see Hannan now, Frank. What'll it be?"

"I'll sign," Frank said calmly.

Hugh only grunted, and Frank looked at him, surprising a look of contempt in his pale eyes. Frank finished shaving then. Hugh tramped over to the bed, picked up the bottle of whiskey from the floor, recovered Jonas's glass, and poured himself a drink of whiskey. He made no conversation, and idly watched while Frank, searching for a clean shirt, finally found Jonas's valise under the bed, and from it unearthed a clean blue shirt.

Frank combed his hair then, and picked up his hat, ready to move. Hugh, starting for the stairs, said, "Better tell the Judge tonight that you and Rhino will be at his office Monday morning to draw the papers."

At the foot of the steps Frank said, "How do you know I won't change my mind, once Virg has cleared me?"

"Why," Hugh said mildly, "nobody's cleared you of killing Pete, have they?"

The rest of it went off quietly, too, so that it seemed as if nothing were happening.

At the Masonic Hall Frank and Virg Moore waited at the top of the stairs while Nunnally went into the hall and, after a moment, returned with Hannan. The sheriff nodded to Frank and looked from him to Moore.

"Hugh said you wanted to see me," Moore said.

"I do," Hannan said. "Do you know where you were between July fourth and ninth?" he asked pleasantly.

"Yeah," Virg said promptly. "On July fifth, I and five other fellas was in the Moab jail."

Hannan grunted. "And the sixth?"

"Still in jail."

"What about the seventh?"

"I camped with Frank."

Hannan showed no sign he was interested in this fact. "The eight, now?"

Moore inclined his head. "With Hugh."

"That right, Hugh?"

"That's right," Nunnally said.

"And you were with Frank the seventh. That right, Frank?"

"If I knew the date, I'd have told you," Frank said, playing his part in this farce.

Hannan was silent a moment, then he asked Moore, "How come you camped with Frank? How do you remember it?"

Moore grinned. "I was supposed to be with Frank all that week. I was kind of throwin' my hat in the door to see if Nunnally had heard about me cuttin' out and gettin' drunk on the Fourth. Frank didn't know because he hadn't seen Nunnally, so I took a chance and saw Hugh the next day."

Frank saw how skillfully Nunnally's alibi for him had been

framed. Virg Moore had been in the Moab jail on the fifth and sixth, as the records, when Hannan wrote for them, would show. There was Moore's word that he was with Frank on the seventh. Since it was impossible for Frank, leaving on the fifth, to ride here and return to Moab by the seventh, Frank could not have killed Rob. The simplicity of it was beautiful and final.

Hannan looked at Frank now and said dryly, "Is he lying? You were afraid he would, remember."

"Not this time," Frank said.

Hannan nodded curtly and said, "It looks like I'm through with you, then, doesn't it?"

Frank nodded and Hannan murmured his thanks to Nunnally and went inside. Hugh grinned meagerly now at Frank and said, "Go have fun," and he and Moore went down the stairs. Inside, the fiddles were sawing away and Dick Afton's hoarse voice was calling the last of a set. *This is the way you turn a corner in your life,* Frank thought bleakly, and went into the hall.

All through supper, which he had with the Judge and the Maases and Carrie, Frank tried to frame a way of telling Carrie about his change of mind regarding Saber. She would welcome it, he thought bitterly. Of her reaction to his taking Rhino Hulst as partner, he wasn't sure, but she must be told tonight.

The opportunity came in the interval between the end of supper and the resumption of the dancing. The Maases and Judge Tavister were deep in a conversation which excluded him and Carrie. They were sitting in the corner contentedly watching the crowd, Carrie's hand resting in his. He said quietly then, "I had a chance to do some thinkin' while I was away, Carrie. I've decided I won't put Saber away. Bedamned to Hannan."

Carrie slowly turned her head to regard him, and he could see the happiness in her eyes. She squeezed his hand in silent token of her approval and happiness.

Frank went on then, in a purposely hesitant voice: "But I'm such a knothead about the money end of it, Carrie. You reckon I should get someone in with me, a partner, say?"

"Yes," Carrie promptly answered. "I know the man, too. Rhino Hulst."

The look of amazement in his face brought a laugh from Carrie. "I know what you've been planning, Frank, but I thought

I'd let you tell me. Dad told me about Rhino coming in to talk over your offer of partnership with him. Dad thinks it's sensible, and so do I."

Frank looked down at her small hand resting in his, and now he tasted the full measure of his defeat. Rhino had been so sure of him that he had gone to the Judge, paving the way for the deal. And the Judge and Carrie approved. The irony of it was too bitter for his taste, and he found a slow anger stirring within him. Couldn't they see what Rhino was after? Of course not, he thought bitterly, and was contrite and wholly glum.

When the music started again, he pulled Carrie to her feet and swung her into the dance. Afterward, he lost track of her. He danced with the girls he had known as a youngster, with their mothers, and he talked with their fathers and with the men he had grown up with, and he found no pleasure in it all. He should never have come, he knew now.

It was much later that he recognized Tess's white dress, and he recalled Jonas. He made his way across the floor to her and took her away from three Horn Creek punchers, and as a waltz began, she settled gently into his arms. Oddly, it was disturbing to touch her, and they didn't speak for a full minute. Presently, Frank glanced down to surprise an expression of utter gravity on her face as she watched the other dancers.

"Not having fun, Tess?" he asked.

She looked up at him searchingly. "I was, until a few minutes ago." She hesitated. "I saw Carrie a moment ago. She said you'd taken a partner for Saber."

Frank felt a hot embarrassment then, and Tess looked away from him. "I wish you well," she said softly.

There was nothing he could reply to that, and they finished out the dance in silence and he left her.

The party began to break up in the small hours of the morning. Families living way up around the Grand Peaks began to leave, the children sleeping in the arms of the menfolk. It was then that Frank remembered he had not told Tess of Jonas.

He mentioned it to Carrie then, and as the dance finished he sent her into the coatroom to tell Tess he would show her across the street. He waited outside the coatroom, standing among the men who were tired and talked out and content, and he felt a leaden discouragement.

When Tess came out, he fell in beside her and they said good night to couples as they made their way across the floor and down the stairs. On the corner, they waited while a spring wagon, Otis Baily driving the team, pulled past them, and Baily called to them, "Good dance, folks. Good night."

The hotel lobby was deserted at this hour. A single dim-lit lamp over the desk was the only light here, and their footsteps echoed loudly in the room.

Frank halted at the foot of the stairs, and Tess mounted the first step and paused. "I'm sorry about Jonas," Frank said stiffly.

Tess looked at him searchingly in the half-darkness, and then she said, "And I'm sorry about you, Frank."

Frank said bitterly, "Tess, I—" he fell silent, desperately wanting to explain himself, and knowing he never could.

"It isn't as if you didn't know him, is it?" Tess asked simply.

"No, I know him."

"Are you that hungry for money?"

"Don't, Tess! Quit it!" Frank said miserably.

"Do you think you'll ever laugh again?" Tess asked then.

He looked imploringly at her, and saw the troubled sweetness in her face. She was waiting for an explanation he could never give. He said obscurely, "Tess, you don't know. Don't be rough, because I can't help it."

"You're afraid of something," Tess said accusingly, and her tone was bitter, too. "I don't like fear in anyone. Especially, I don't like it in you. Good night, Frank."

She turned, and he watched her go up the stairs, and somehow it seemed the most important thing in the world at the moment that she should turn and come back and tell him in her easy friendly way that it didn't matter. But she didn't. She vanished at the top of the stairs and he stood there a full minute, oddly without hope, before he turned and went out.

Chapter 15

AFTER FRANK AND NUNNALLY HAD GONE, Jonas lay awake in the darkness of John's room staring at the ceiling. His mind was fogged with alcohol and his head ached blazingly, but there was no mistaking the words he had just heard. Hugh's blow had stunned him, but it had not driven consciousness from him— and he had heard something not intended for him.

He rose unsteadily to his feet now and listened. The last faint sound of their footsteps died, and now he took a slow turn around the dark room. His head throbbed solidly and it was an effort to think, but he reviewed Hugh's words, trying to read meaning into them. Frank Chess had killed somebody called Pete, someone who worked for Rhino, and knowledge of this was being used by Rhino and Hugh to blackmail Frank into signing something.

Pete who? he wondered. He recalled the men who worked for Rhino and then it suddenly came to him. Pete Faraday, that damned Ute half-breed, of course.

Now he went out into the other room and poured himself a drink of whiskey and stood motionless, a gray foreboding touching him. He liked Frank and always had, and he found himself examining the reasons why he should. He had discounted the current story of Frank's mother, for he had worked around animals long enough to know that a good breed does not come from worthless stock. And he accepted all the stories of Frank's reckless ways without feeling any censure, because those ways had never hurt anyone. People like himself, Jonas thought, drudged their way out of mediocrity and acquired a liking for people and a kind of trust of them on the way, but Frank had never needed that. There was a deep and careless generosity in him that was as much a part of him as his gentle mockery and his heedless love of fun. He was gay and quick and easy; he could break any woman's heart, and he didn't know that he could, and he was too honest to care, even if he did know. Frank was a man who gave everything and he should get everything, Jonas thought without any envy, and now he was being milked by Rhino.

Jonas cursed Rhino and Nunnally then in an impassioned whisper. The two of them were like a blight, killing everything they touched, and even if Jonas hadn't liked Frank, he would have wanted to help him now.

But murder was murder, even if a dog like Pete Faraday was the man who was murdered. A sensible caution that alcohol could not entirely dim told Jonas to stay out of this.

He sat down on the edge of the bed now, thinking laboriously of this. The more he thought, the more he knew he didn't want any part in this. The thing to do was stay here, and not even go back to the dance. No use risking Hugh's suspicion that he might have overheard the conversation. Tess could get home easily enough, and there were enough men there to show her fun. *I don't know anything,* he thought.

And then it all went sour deep inside him, and he felt an obscure guilt. Frank was in trouble and needed help, and Jonas was backing out of it.

Jonas shook his head and lay down. It was all too confusing, and his head hurt and he'd had too much to drink. He felt sleep coming like an avalanche to envelop him now, and he welcomed it.

When he awakened next morning the sun was high. He sat up and his head felt as if it were loaded with loose shot that rolled around at his every movement. Slowly, then, the events of last night came back to him, and remembering it all, the feeling of guilt returned.

He rose now and doused his face with cold water, then stripped out of his clothes and put on a worn pair of denim pants. After that he shaved unsteadily. Today he would ride out to O-Bar to begin work tomorrow, but first, of course, he must see Tess and square things for last night.

But his mind kept returning to Frank. *All right, I tell him I heard and what does he do?* Jonas thought. He couldn't answer that. If Frank was being blackmailed, then it meant that he must have murdered Faraday, and what could he, Jonas, do about that? Nothing. The kindest thing to do was to keep Frank's secret for him.

Once that was settled, Jonas finished shaving, climbed into his shirt, picked up his hat and went out. At the foot of the stairs, he paused and looked over at the freight yard. It was locked up tight, boarded shut; the sight of it brought a quiet curse to his lips.

He got breakfast, and while he was eating, he heard the church bell ringing, signifying church was out. Afterward, he strolled back toward the hotel, meeting a few stiffly dressed people taking the quiet main street home from church.

At the hotel, he waved to Mr. Newhouse behind the desk and climbed the stairs to Tess's room. Her door was open, and he knocked softly on the frame and was bid enter.

He tramped in and saw Tess at the open window. She had been leaning out, and now she turned to see who it was. She was dressed in a dark suit that made her hair seem pale as taffy and she was, Jonas thought, utterly beautiful. And not for him. She smiled at him and looked out the window again and then said, "I smell a change in the weather, Jonas."

"If I looked at the sky, my head would roll off," Jonas said gloomily. "How are you, Tess?"

"Sort of sleepy." She came back into the room and lifted some things from the lone armchair, motioned Jonas into it and seated herself on the bed.

Jonas sat down and regarded her uncomfortably. "I'm sorry about last night, Tess. I just went to sleep over in my room."

Tess grinned tolerantly. "Maybe that's the best thing that could have happened to you."

Jonas made a wry face. "I make a hell of a cut-up."

Tess really laughed then, and Jonas grinned crookedly.

"How'd you get home?" Jonas asked.

"Frank brought me," Tess said.

A shadow seemed to cross her face then, and Jonas, noticing it, wondered. He said, "Did Frank have fun?"

"Yes, he was celebrating, too," Tess said. There was something in her voice that made Jonas look curiously at her.

Tess, seeing it, said, in explanation, "He was celebrating his partnership. I guess it's no secret."

"Partnership in what?"

"Partnership in Saber. With Rhino."

Jonas sat motionless several seconds, and he felt something like a cold touch of wind that raised the hair on his neck. Saber was what Frank was going to sign away. This was the blackmail. Jonas thought of that with a deep, shocked soberness, remembering Saber's vast acres.

He was silent so long that Tess said, "Well, doesn't that mean anything to you, Jonas?"

Jonas said slowly, "No. Why should it?"

"If Frank's Rhino's partner, he'll tell him our freeze-out scheme."

"Don't you believe it," Jonas said promptly.

"He's afraid of something," Tess said, with a strange bitterness. "I don't trust frightened people."

"Who said he was?" Jonas asked curiously.

Tess looked at him wonderingly. "I do. It's in his face, for the world to see. You can't loathe a man one day and then take him in as partner the next unless you're afraid of him. Or unless he knows something you're afraid of having known."

Jonas's glance slid away from her face, and he studied the pattern on the carpet. She had come close enough to the truth, with nothing but her intuition, to make him uncomfortable. For a moment, he considered telling her the truth. Perhaps the two of them could work something out. And then he knew that was wrong; nobody but Frank himself could work anything out. And it was even more imperative, now that he knew the stakes in this game, to keep silent.

He rose now and said stubbornly, "Frank won't tell Rhino about our scheme. You know how you can prove it?"

"Yes. If I still have a job at the end of next week."

Jonas nodded. "That's right." He picked up his hat now, and walked toward the door. "How's the freightin' business goin', Tess?"

"Not so well," Tess said, and she smiled faintly. "I wish you'd stayed in business long enough to haul that two-ton pump from Leadville to Meeker for the Esmeralda people."

Jonas grinned. "So you got that job, did you? Why, it's a

107

cinch. You knock down—" He paused, as Tess raised her hand to stop him.

She looked at Jonas now and smiled, and he understood.

"What I don't know, I can't be blamed for not knowing, can I?" Tess asked.

Jonas grinned and stuck out his hand, and Tess took it. "Well, bad luck to your business, Tess," he said now. "When it gets so bad it looks good for us, you know where to find me."

When Jonas was gone, Tess strolled back to the window and looked pensively at the street. She could see the McGarritys' yard now, as bare of activity as a graveyard. She wished, suddenly, passionately, that she had as much confidence in Frank Chess as Jonas did. His words of last night had haunted her all day, and she would never forget the tortured shame that was in his face as she left him last night. Somehow, fear didn't fit him, nor did inarticulate apologies, nor pleading.

Why do I care? she thought angrily, turning away from the window. Why did she? He'd be married to Carrie Tavister soon, and she would shape him into the same dull, dry, gray kind of a man that her father was, cautious and taciturn and proper. By then he would be a fitting partner for Rhino, and the two of them, one with a respectable front and connections, the other with a ruthless cunning, would make undreamed-of fortunes. Only she would miss Frank's gay, happy-go-lucky way, his mockery and impudence, his fun and his careless friendliness. She found herself standing there, hands fisted, muscles tense in protest.

She shook her head and relaxed then, and set about her Sunday routine. She had dinner with Mr. Newhouse, and afterward came back to her room and wrote some letters, washed some things, and did some sewing. In late afternoon, she noticed that the sun had gone under the clouds. They weren't the black, billowy clouds of the summer thunderstorms common to this high country; they were pale and uniform and spread over all the sky, betokening a long break in the weather.

Restless now, she took up a light shawl then and went downstairs and outside, turning toward the river in the beginning dusk. The McGarritys' as she passed it looked as if it had been vacant for years. At the river, she turned downstream, walking slowly along the riverbank. As she passed the rear of the horse lot, she thought again of Frank. Tomorrow noon, he could be Rhino's partner, and she wondered if the partnership would include the lot, too. Carrie had told her they were signing the agreement Monday morning.

When it began to grow dark, she turned back, retracing her steps. It was almost dark when she again passed the horse lot, and by the time she reached the side street, it was full dark.

This time, she took the cinder walk that led past the McGarritys' and traveled past the high board fence. Passing the gate now she glanced over at the heavy chain and padlock. As she passed, between the crack in the two halves of the gate, the merest flicker of light came to her. She walked on several steps, thinking it might be the reflection on the padlock from the lights of the town up ahead. And then she halted, wondering.

Coming back now, she put her head to the crack between the gates and peered inside. It was dark; she had imagined it. But just as she was ready to turn away, she saw a light. It seemed as if it came from the far stable, and might be the dim light of a lantern seen briefly as the door was opened and closed.

Tess stood there a moment, puzzled. It was doubtless some of the town kids who knew the yard was closed and accordingly had moved in to play there. But a careless lantern around a stable was dangerous.

She backed away and considered. Both John and Jonas were away, and she was more or less responsible for that, so it was up to her to handle this.

There was enough tomboy still in Tess for the fence not to bother her. She moved back to the corner, and then followed the fence along the side. Presently, she came to a stack of empty crates piled against the fence. Climbing them carefully, she achieved the top of the fence and waited a moment, looking at the stable. Through one of the cracks, the dim light was visible again.

She let herself down on the inside of the fence until she was hanging by her hands, and then lightly dropped the last foot. Cautiously now, but not afraid, she made her way past the open wagon sheds towards the stable. Whoever these kids were, they were going to be surprised, she promised herself.

As she approached the stable, she heard the low murmur of voices—and they were not the voices of children. Softly, then, she moved against the slab stable and found a knothole through which she could look.

There was a lantern turned down dim on the stable's dirt floor. Sitting with his back to her was a man she instantly recognized as Bill Schulte. He was in the act of tilting a bottle in his mouth, but his body hid the figure beyond. The second man was lying on some hay, and there were dirty dishes scattered about him.

Bill Schulte finished his drink, and rose, and then Tess saw that the man lying beyond was Pete Faraday. His shirt was off, and there was a dirty bandage on his right shoulder.

She heard Bill Schulte say now, "Want anything?"

"Gimme a drink, Bill," Faraday asked.

"Not to no Injun. You'd be singing in twenty minutes."

Faraday moved restlessly. "When do I get out of here? This ain't no place to stay."

Bill laughed and shoved the bottle in his hip pocket. "I dunno," he said now. "When Rhino says so."

"Ask him how long tomorrow."

"All right. You all set?"

"Leave the lantern."

"No. Somebody might see it and there'd be hell to pay."

Schulte picked up the lantern, kicked the dirty tin plates aside and said, "I'll be movin'."

Tess backed away then and slowly retraced her steps. When she heard the door creak open, she froze in the darkness. Schulte, however, took the fence closest to town. She saw the dim bulk of his figure on the fence, heard the thud as he dropped to the ground, and then there was silence.

Once she was over the fence and on the ground again, she walked slowly toward the hotel. Pete Faraday was hurt, apparently, and Rhino was keeping him hidden. For what reason she couldn't begin to guess, and sensibly she decided she wouldn't even try. But the fact remained that Jonas ought to know it.

Back in her room, she sat down and wrote a note in pencil:

Jonas:
    Pete Faraday is hurt and Rhino is hiding him in the stable of your yard. Tell me what you want me to do.
                                                    Tess

She addressed it to Jonas in a sealed envelope, and downstairs she left it at the desk with instructions to give it to the first O-Bar hand who happened in. Afterward, she went in to supper, and when she came out later, the note was gone. It had been given to a Slash-H hand almost immediately.

Next day, Tess almost wished that Rhino would fire her. The mail, which Shinner brought in at nine o'clock, held a torrent of letters, mostly abusive, addressed to Manager, Hulst Freight Lines. Among them were complaints of stations passed up by freight wagons, demands for payment of damages for wreckage incurred by a drunken Hulst teamster at one of the mountain stations, a frantic demand from the Leadville agent for more wagons, and a dirty penciled note from a teamster broken down on the road asking for a new front wheel and a kingbolt. This last had been brought by the mail driver who had passed the wreck.

Tess spent the rest of the day answering the letters, trying to start the week's schedule, and rounding up reluctant teamsters in Hugh Nunnally's and Rhino's absence. Rhino came in smiling in midafternoon and left immediately. Sometime later in the afternoon, a slow rain began to fall.

She was working on the last of the answers long after five o'clock when a puncher, his slicker dripping water, laid a sodden note on her desk and touched his hat and went out.

Tess opened the envelope and took out her own note to Jonas. On the back of it was written:

Tess:
 That's what Frank's been scared of. Tell him. He won't sign now.

Jonas

Tess read the note and a wild elation came to her. She rose, now, a frantic urgency within her. And then she sat down slowly. It was too late. The agreement was signed this morning. Nobody had told her it had been, but the look on Rhino's face when he came in today was enough. It was too late, she was too late, everything was too late. For no good reason she began to cry then, and this was the only sound in the quiet office.

Chapter 16

THE RAIN was falling steadily and implacably for the third day when Frank rode into the last meadows near Saber nestling snugly against the black timber at the far end of them. A curtain of low smoke hung over the buildings. The peaks to the east were lost in gray and heavy clouds, and the valley running north was half invisible through the shifting streamers of mist.

Under his leg in the rifle boot, he felt the faint ridges of his fishing rod; it had not been out of the boot since he'd left town Monday, after the signing. Rhino had suggested, and Frank had been thankful for it, that he should stay away from Saber the few days it took to get the old crew moved out. Frank had no stomach for making that announcement to them, and having to eat his own words of a week ago; he'd been glad enough for Nunnally to break the news and pay the crew off with a ten-dollar bonus per man. He had gone fishing, and for the past two days he had paced Ed Hanley's vacant shack, while the rain turned Roan Creek muddy and wild. Idleness and boredom—and finally skeptical curiosity—had driven him home, for he was anxious to see how his new crew had shaped up. For part of the agreement, and written into it, was that he was to handle the cattle end of Saber. This was his own, to stick with and nurse and watch grow until, maybe in the spring, Carrie would believe he was serious, and they would marry.

He off-saddled, stabled his horse in the big barn, and forked down a generous amount of hay, and then stood in the barn door looking over the ranch. This place, he thought narrowly, was forever spoiled for him. When he and Carrie married, they would build a new house away from here.

A pair of punchers, unknown to him, lounged in the door of the bunkhouse, watching him. He got his rod and tramped past the bunkhouse toward his room. He nodded to the two punchers, and they nodded curtly in return. No smoke was coming from the office stove, he noted.

112

Once in his room, he changed into dry boots, knowing what his next move would be. He'd never seen Rhino's entire crew, and he wanted a look at them, and behind that wish lay a deep skepticism. They would be trash. *But that's part of the bargain,* he told himself grimly.

He tramped back to the bunkhouse and stepped inside. Here, around the big center table with its overhead kerosene lamp lighted against the gray day, eight or ten men were lounging. Half of them were engaged in a desultory poker game, and when he halted just inside the door, they regarded him in silence. He had seen most of these men before, but he knew the names of only two of them, Morg Lister and Albie Beecham. Albie was standing at the foot of the table outside the circle of light cast by the lamp, a small, wiry little man with an inner viciousness stamped in every lineament of his ravaged face. His eyes glinted with malice at the sight of Frank now.

Morg Lister was seated at the far side of the table, the greasy deck of cards in his hand. His sallow and taciturn face was expressionless, blank with stupidity. Frank took a deep breath, and because someone had to speak, he said, pleasantly enough, "Howdy, Lister."

Morg grunted a greeting, and Frank came into the room. "Where's Hugh?" he asked.

"Ridin'."

"I supposed he was," Frank said, still pleasantly. "Where, though?"

"He'll be back in a couple of days," Morg said evasively.

Frank sized up the rest of the crew with a slow, searching stare, gauging their temper. It was totally sour, totally suspicious. He said now, "Did Hugh tell off a crew for me?"

Lister looked around at the others, who shrugged, and then he glanced at Frank. It was Albie who answered, though, in a wry, aggressive voice, "He wasn't expectin' you back."

Frank looked carefully at him, and then at Lister. "All right. Four of you ride out with me tomorrow, then."

The men glanced uneasily at each other, and now looked at Morg, who seemed to be the spokesman. Lister said, "We can't do that. We're takin' orders from Hugh, and he told us to stick here."

"And do what?"

"Wait for the horses comin' up from the lot."

A faint temper edged into Frank's eyes now, and he checked it. There was no sense in quarreling with this sorry crew until it was plain in everybody's mind as to who was working for him. After that, he would have his way with them, or they would not work here.

He turned then and went out, pausing undecided on the doorstep. Then he buttoned his slicker and moved off through the rain toward the barn and the outbuildings, no certain destination in mind. He wanted a look at all the gear lying around the place now. Some of the old Saber crew had been here so long that it had doubtless been difficult to sort the ranch stuff from theirs. At memory of the old crew, and of this sorry lot in the bunkhouse, his lip curled in contempt. Riffraff, every man of them, loyal to Rhino and Hugh through God knew what kinds of blackmail and debts. *The same as I am,* he thought bittterly.

Their refusal to discuss Hugh's whereabouts, however, was puzzling. Lister had evaded his question and the others had volunteered nothing, and he wondered what sort of errand would take Hugh and part of his crew out in weather like this.

He prowled through the blacksmith shop, and noted that Cass, probably out of an understandable spite, had helped himself to the better tools. He didn't blame him.

Turning now to look back at the bunkhouse in the fading light, he saw a slickered puncher lounging in the open door of the barn, watching him. The puncher moved back inside as Frank turned. He was being watched, apparently, and the crew must have arrived collectively at this decision, since there was no leader among them. Frank turned this over in his mind now, remembering the suspicion with which they greeted him, remembering, too, Albie's announcement that Hugh hadn't expected him back so soon.

Now, he cruised on past the open-face wagon shed. There was a light spring wagon missing, which surely wouldn't have been claimed by the old Saber crew. Without pausing, Frank picked out the wagon's wheel tracks; they swung close to the corral, where the team was harnessed, then cut out north, where they were soon blurred by what Frank read as the tracks of a half-dozen horses heading in the same direction. Hugh, apparently, had needed a wagon on his errand.

Frank was cruising around the corrals as the triangle clanged for supper. When, later, he took his place at the table in the cookshack he saw that Hugh had dug up an aged Chinese cook for the crew. The cook spoke to none of them, and they did not speak to him, and his food was wretched.

After supper, Frank went back to his room. Once there, he rolled a cigarette and pondered what he had seen this afternoon. The crew wasn't going to let him out of its sight. On the other hand, they didn't seem worried enough to send a man to Hugh to warn him that Frank was back.

That left the door wide open, and Frank was going to take advantage of it. With a headstart in the morning, he could follow the wagon tracks at a pace that would put miles between him and the crew before his absence was noticed.

It was an hour before daylight when he wakened and dressed in the chill darkness. He heard the soft murmur of the persistent rain on the roof, and he swore mildly; if it had held all night, the tracks of Hugh's wagon might be washed away.

Letting himself out, he skirted the bunkhouse widely, thankful that the ranch dog had been appropriated by one of the departing Saber crew.

In the barn he lighted the lantern just long enough to saddle his horse, and afterward he rode out toward the north. Until daylight came, he concentrated on putting as much distance between himself and the ranch as he could. The valley curved in a great crescent to the east along the timbered base of the peaks, and when it swung north again it had lifted to the high aspens. On the hunch that Hugh's business lay in the high country, Frank short cut the long valley road, cutting straight to the far point of the crescent, and keeping to the narrow trails through the dripping black timber that he had memorized from childhood.

In midmorning he came onto the upper Elk at the high meadow where he had first gathered his horses for Fort Crawford. Carefully then, Frank rode the bank of the stream, watching for the wagon tracks. He found them in the middle of the meadow; the wheels had gouged furrows in the turf of the stream bank, and they pointed north still.

He reined in and folded his arms on the saddle horn and

115

looked off toward the north, considering this. Saber range ran on for some miles beyond this meadow, but it was upended country of poor grass that Saber hands had cursed every round-up. Each year, a few cattle strayed into its tangle of brushy canyons where they had to be pried out by dogged searching. There was little water back there, for this chunk of country drained the boulder-fields that spent water as fast as it fell. It was the sort of dark corner Hugh Nunnally would hunt up, but the fact that he knew of its existence and was using it baffled Frank.

He went on now, climbing a sharp hogback and dropping down into a boulder-strewn canyon bed running an inch of murky water across its ten-foot width.

He followed this a little way and again picked up the wagon tracks as they crawled out of it, labored over a flinty ridge, and slid down into another rocky wash flanked with a tangle of brush. As he went deeper and deeper into this country, he tried to puzzle this out, and could not.

It was around noon when he heard the chunking of an axe somewhere ahead. Reining up, he tried to place the sound, and as he listened another axe joined in. Putting his horse into motion now, he rode up the wash that was close-hedged by brush.

Presently, the brush broke away for a steep cliff, and rounding it, Frank saw the wagon ahead of him. Hugh Nunnally, in a soggy yellow slicker, was standing by the wagon in the rain watching two punchers, slickerless and drenched to the skin, who were lugging a fresh-cut pine post past him and into the wide mouth of a canyon. Frank knew this canyon, although it had always gone nameless. It trailed back for two or three miles, giving scanty forage to stock, before its dry wash began to show water. This water came from a spring at the head of the canyon that was backed up against the peaks, but the water soon disappeared in the sand. Nunnally, Frank saw now, was directing the fencing of the canyon mouth.

He urged his horse forward now, and in moving the horse kicked a rock. Hugh's head turned quickly. When he saw a rider, his hand clawed at his slicker, striving for the gun under it, and then it ceased movement, as he recognized Frank.

A blazing anger crawled into Hugh's broad face now, and he turned and walked toward Frank. His slicker was soaked through, his arms muddy to the elbows, and his boots were caked with mud.

"Who sent you up here?" he asked meagerly.

"Nobody," Frank observed mildly. The two men looked at each other, and Frank read the wild wrath in Nunnally's pale eyes.

Hugh said then, his voice almost normal, "I thought you'd gone off for a week's fishin'."

"All the streams are muddy," Frank said idly. He looked over at the pole fence strung halfway across the canyon. The crew had seen now; they stood silent, drenched and muddy, looking at Hugh. Ed Hanley, Frank noticed, was among them.

Hugh called to them now, "All right, knock off for grub, boys." He turned to look up at Frank now, and his face was contained, amiable once more.

"Rush job?" Frank asked.

Hugh almost smiled, "No, these jugheads are goin' to learn to work, once more. There's plenty of it around here, too."

Frank considered asking why it was necessary to work in this weather at a job unpleasant enough any time, but he held his question.

Hugh said now, "Anything special on your mind?" in an offhand way that somehow lacked the casualness it was intended to carry.

"Yeah. A crew. They didn't have orders back at the ranch to work for me, so I came to you."

Hugh looked at the wagon thoughtfully. The crew had stored dry wood under the wagon; now they were building a small fire under the wagon out of the rain, stamping their feet in the thin, cold drizzle and watching Nunnally.

Hugh shook his head slowly. "Frank, you came too soon. I'm goin' to need every man-jack of them for a few more days, and I counted on your bein' gone." He scowled thoughtfully at Frank. "Look, help a man out, will you?"

"All right."

"I left a dozen things hangin' fire down at the lot that Rhino can't settle. Get something to eat here, and then ride on down to town, will you? When you get back, I'll give you a crew."

Frank nodded. It was plain enough that Nunnally wanted him out of the way, the quicker and farther away the better.

Hugh tramped over toward the wagon, and Frank dismounted and led his horse after him.

The men at the fire nodded in greeting, and Frank came to a halt, nodding too. His glance traveled to Ed Hanley, squatting on his haunches warming his hands against the small flame. They regarded each other a brief second, each remembering their last meeting, and then Hanley said, "Howdy, Frank."

Frank spoke to him, accepting the tin plate of half-warmed mulligan Hugh gave him. While he ate, Hugh enumerated the items he wanted Frank to pass on to Rhino. Any hay bought from Grannigan downriver was to be turned back, or if already paid for, destroyed, since it contained loco weed. All horses destined for Carpenter at Leadville were to be shod before delivery. There were other things of this nature, none of them really urgent, and Frank memorized them as he ate.

Finished with his coffee, he set the tin cup in the wagon bed, buttoned up his slicker, and tramped over to his horse. Hugh followed him, and watched him mount.

"I'm much obliged, Frank," Hugh said. "Don't worry about your crew. Once we have the horses moved and some things cleaned up, you'll have your pick."

Frank rode out then. When he was only a few minutes gone, he heard the axe chunking again. Hugh was in a hurry to finish the corral, apparently, and Frank wondered why. It was illogical that the horses from the lot that Lister was waiting for were destined for this canyon. The sheer trouble of getting them in and out of here made Frank discount that possibility. Yet Morg was waiting for the horses today, and Hugh was driving his crew to finish the fence.

By the time Frank had reached Elk Creek again, his mind was made up. Instead of taking the short cut back to Saber, he clung to the big crescent meadow, and in the midafternoon he came across the bunch of horses the crew were driving ahead of them.

Lister was riding swing on the bunch of a hundred-odd horses; at sight of him, Lister pulled away and rode over to meet him.

"You sure turn out early," Lister said sullenly. He was watching Frank's face carefully.

Frank nodded. "I found Hugh, and we'll pick a crew when he's through. I'm on my way to town."

118

Lister scowled, pondering this. The suspicion on the man's face was transparent, but Frank's statement that he had talked with Hugh confounded him. He said, "Hugh send you to town?"

Frank said, "Ask him," and moved on past the herd. He rode some distance before he turned in the saddle to look back at them. The herd moved on, Lister with them, and counting the riders, he knew Lister had not dropped a man out to follow him. Once there was timber between him and the herd, he rode on a way farther, and then cut into the timber. He had been seen by the crew and his errand established, which was what he wanted. Presently, he found the trail he had taken this morning, and he turned back up it in the direction of the aspen meadow.

Arriving there, he left his horse well back in the timber and made his way slowly through the thick aspens until he had a view of the meadow. Picking the driest spot here, he settled down to watch.

It was several minutes before he discovered the man huddled under the three pine trees by the corral where Frank had once camped. This man was waiting too; he tramped restlessly among the trees, smoking incessantly, occasionally sitting down until his restlessness drove him to his feet again. It was another half-hour before Frank heard the shrill whistles of the crew hazing the horses up into the meadow. The man under the trees moved toward the corral and opened the gate, then stood there, waving and whistling.

The first of the horses came into sight then, and the point rider turned them toward the corral. Once they were inside, the gate was swung shut and the riders collected under the trees. They built a fire and then settled down around it, and they too were waiting. So far, there was nothing significant in this, Frank thought. He shifted his position now, seeking a drier spot. There was more to come, he knew, and he hoped it would not be dark before it happened.

He waited another half-hour, cursing the darkening afternoon. In a short while it would be too dark to see anything. Water trickled down his neck, and his feet, soaking wet, were so cold they were numb.

He looked up then to see one of the punchers under the tree run out across the stream and pause in the meadow, head turned toward the mountains. The man raised a hand for silence, and Frank knew he was listening. Then he beckoned the others to him, so as to get them away from the noise of the stream. In a group, they stood motionless, listening. Then they waited.

It was another five minutes before a band of horses broke out of the trail from the peaks. They came boiling down off the trail and into the meadow in scattered formation, and made for the creek. Some of them started to graze immediately. All of them, Frank noticed, had mud-caked legs and bellies. And then he saw the three riders come off the trail now on weary, jaded horses. They rode straight up to the waiting crew, and there was a short parley. Half of Rhino's crew now went back for their horses, mounted, and started bunching up the new herd that was scattered over the meadow.

Frank regarded these horses carefully, but they were too far away for him to identify their brands. There were about a hundred of them, and they looked travel-beaten and footsore, their tails burred and their heads down. But they were a good bunch of horses. They could have come, he knew, only from over the mountains by any of the old Indian trails.

Now half Rhino's bunch started hazing the new horses north over the hogback. The horses went reluctantly, for they were almost beat, and now Frank knew why Hugh had been in such a hurry to finish the corral. He had expected these horses, who were being hidden out in the canyon back there.

Frank watched the rest of the crew mount now, while one man ran to the corral and opened the gate. Rhino's horses were hazed out now, and roughly divided into two groups. One group was chased up the trail the other horses had just come down. The other bunch was driven back and forth across the meadow, and each time they were turned around they moved closer to the hogback.

Frank stared at this in bafflement. Once this bunch was close to the hogback, they were turned and driven clear across the meadow and onto a trail leading over to Horn Creek. They were gone only a few minutes, when they were driven back. Now the back-and-forth process was resumed again. The horses were driven ceaselessly, always bunched. Frank's glance shifted to the three riders who had come in with the last bunch; they were squatted around the fire, resting.

120

The horses caught his attention again. They had been driven over to the head of the trail now, where they were made to mill round and round.

Frank watched this with growing bafflement. Suddenly, it came to him with the weight of utter conviction. *They're covering the tracks of the bunch that came over the peaks.*

It made sense. Half the bunch sent up the trail would blot out the tracks on the trail. This bunch here, having been driven back and forth in the meadow and down every trail that led onto it, had left a thousand confusing tracks of their own and covered every track of the last bunch. In an hour the rain would leach out the sharp edges of all these tracks, making identification of any single horse impossible. Anyone trailing these horses over the mountains would come to the meadow and find thousands of blurred horse tracks going in all directions, and Rhino's band of a hundred horses would be innocently grazing here.

He settled back on his heels now, and slowly rubbed a hand across his face. He had the answer to a lot of things now. Rhino, his partner, was dealing in stolen horses. With Saber's vast range, he could hide the stolen stuff until they were vent-branded or their brands altered and healed. The set-up was foolproof. Nobody ever questioned a Saber-branded horse, and any number of horses could be brought in over the back door of the peaks.

He saw how carefully Rhino had planned and executed this, so sure of himself that these horses had been stolen and scheduled to arrive here weeks before Frank knew he was after Saber. No wonder Rhino had suggested the fishing trip, and no wonder the old Saber crew was promptly moved out. No wonder—

"Getting an eyeful, Pretty Boy?"

The voice was wry and gibing, coming from behind him. Even as he turned his head, still squatting in the brush, he knew who had spoken.

Albie Beecham stood there in the slow rain, gun in hand and cocked. He had taken off his slicker so its noise would not give him away, and he had come up within a dozen feet of Frank before he spoke.

Frank came carefully erect and turned, his hands at his sides. He was caught cold, and he saw the bitter exultation in Albie's vicious face.

"It took all day, but I made it," Albie said thinly.

Frank didn't comment.

"So now you know," Albie jeered, "and now you're dead."

A cold swift fear touched Frank then. Was he going to shoot him, now? *Not without Nunnally's word,* Frank thought. But the promise was there, naked and cold, so plain the crew already knew it. Once he discovered Rhino's business, he was dead. They'd used him and now they were through with him. His discovery here, coupled with what he had seen today, would earn him a bullet in the back.

He had been cold before; now he was sweating. He beat his mind for some way out of this, watching Albie with a narrow attention. If he moved, Albie would shoot. Even if Albie missed him, this would bring the crew from the meadow here in a minute's time. And then it came to him and he didn't like it, but he knew he was going to do it.

He smiled with an easy confidence and put out his hand. "Give it to me, Albie. It's no use."

Albie's gun steadied on him.

Frank took a step toward him, a slow step, his hand still extended, and now he raised his other hand slowly to push his hat off his forehead. He looked beyond Albie and called sharply, "Jonas, get closer—and be quiet. The meadow's full of them."

Albie had the hint. He acted promptly, wisely, because he was almost sure—but only almost—that Frank was bluffing, and that there was nobody behind him. He raised his gun shoulder high and fired a shot for help. That was the most Frank had hoped for.

He wrenched off his hat and threw it at Albie's head, hoping to distract his aim, and lunged for the slight puncher. Albie's shot bellowed almost in his face, but it was too late and Frank was on him. His head butted Albie's chest and his long arms were around him.

Albie, cursing wildly, went down, and Frank fell atop him and clamped onto his gun. They wrestled silently, viciously for seconds in the muddy leaves, Frank holding Albie's gun in an iron grip as they rolled over and over. It took Frank a few experimental seconds to discover that, once Albie was pinned on his back, his own extra weight could pin him down. Albie's arm was wrapped around Frank's neck, and he hugged Frank with a wild and stubborn tenacity. With a cold and wicked haste upon him now, Frank read Albie's motives. Albie wanted to hold him until help from the meadow got here, and it was surely on the way.

Smothering Albie with his weight now, Frank clawed at his slicker with his right hand, trying to open it and get his gun. The stout buckles held, and he moved his hand to the pocket and ripped it savagely. His face was mashed against Albie's chest, and now Albie, reading Frank's intent, tightened his hold and rolled Frank over on one side, pinning his free hand under his body. This was too slow, Frank knew, and a wild desperation came to him. He must break, and soon.

He opened his mouth now and sank his teeth savagely into Albie's shoulder. Albie howled, and his hug loosened. He heaved over on his other side with a violence that rolled Frank off him and tore his grip from the wet gun in Albie's right hand.

But Albie's very violence wrenched the gun from his own hand too. It fell and skidded in the mud beyond Frank's head. Frank rolled over, his legs driving in the mud to bring him to his feet, but Albie was already lunging for the gun, and Frank knew they must repeat their struggle. He ignored Albie's gun and, kneeling now, he ripped at the inside of his slicker pocket with a violence that almost tore out his nails. The oilskin gave, and now his hand drove down for the gun in the waistband of his denims, just as Albie stumbled and fell on the muddy gun and picked it up.

Frank saw him swing it in a tight arc toward him, struggling with his muddy hand to pull back the slippery hammer. His thumb slipped, and now Frank's gun came up. Albie had his left hand flat, streaking for the hammer to palm it back, when Frank shot. Albie, kneeling too, was knocked over as if some invisible hand had swept him to the ground, and his left hand, still traveling its course, slapped into the hammer and the gun went off in the air.

Frank was aware of several things now as he rose. There was a pounding of horses at full run in the meadow. He was still screened from the meadow by the aspens, and he knew he had not been seen. If he could get out of here now—but no, there was Albie. *But maybe Albie's dead,* he thought.

123

Swiftly, then, Frank searched for and found his hat, looked briefly around the scuffed leaves and mud for anything he had dropped, and then ran for Albie.

Albie, drenched and muddy, lay on his face. His shot, Frank saw, had caught Albie in the chest, and he was dead already. Frank plunged past him now into the timber, and as he ran he heard a horse crashing through the brush behind him, and a man yelled, "Where are you?"

Frank lay face down, listening, his heart pumping wildly. The rider moved on then, calling in the deepening dusk to his companions. Frank rose and ran, and when he came to the trail he turned down it. A horse shied away from him in this wet, twilight gloom, and he knew it was Albie's mount. He ran on a few yards, and came to his own horse.

Mounting, he heard behind him a shout, and then three quick shots in succession. They had discovered Albie. Frank pulled his horse around and roweled him down the trail. Behind him now, he could hear other horses coming down the trail at a dead run.

He yanked his pony off the trail then, turning him into the close timber. Lying flat on his pony's neck, he gave him his head, and rode blindly for several minutes, branches clawing at him as he rode under them. Reining up then in a stand of dripping pine, he turned to listen. He could hear nothing, and he knew it was too dark now for them to track any more.

He was free, and he speculated on what that meant. Nobody had seen him, so nobody would know who killed Albie. The persistent rain would make identification of his tracks or his horse's tracks, hopeless. When last seen by any of Rhino's crew, he was miles back in the crescent meadow on his way to town. He could bluff this through, claiming innocence of any knowledge of Albie's death. If he ran now, everything was lost —Carrie, Saber, his whole future.

And then he saw the flaw. *Hugh will check on the time I got to town, and I'll have five hours to account for.* He thought of that with a narrow pessimism, reading his defeat in it.

And then the answer came to him, and he turned it over slowly and carefully in his mind. Normally, leaving Hugh when he did, he would have reached town at six. Rhino would be gone, the lot closed, with perhaps someone, probably Tess, working in the office.

Then it was up to Tess. If he could find Tess tonight, get her to write in her own handwriting the items Hugh had given him for Rhino, go to the office and leave this list on Rhino's desk tonight, so that it would be there first thing in the morning, the plan would work. Provided, of course, that he could get to town without being seen, so that Tess would say he had come in just as she was closing last night.

He put his horse into motion now, and rode on in the darkness, and he was remembering Tess's words of Saturday night. Shrewdly, he knew she would not have spoken those words unless she liked him. Yes, he could count on Tess.

He rode now with a purpose.

Chapter 17

HANNAN LEANED BACK to light his cigar, and over the match flame he saw Doc Breathit's ruddy face grinning. There was a friendly malice in Doc's eyes, and he said now, with derision, "She gave it to you. She folded so you wouldn't cry."

"I was ready to," Hannan agreed. He looked across the table at Tess's big stack of chips, then raised his glance to her and grinned. She smiled back, but it was a warning smile.

Newhouse, to his left, riffled the cards impatiently. "Take off that star and see what she does to you, Buck. You're afraid to."

"That's the way he get votes," Isaac Maas said gently from around his big calabash pipe. He scratched his thick black hair and said: "Simple. You lose enough pots to people and they feel grateful enough to vote for you. What they think of your brains, I won't go into."

Tess winked at Hannan, and he laughed. She liked these people and she liked these evenings of poker in Mr. Newhouse's living room on the hotel's ground floor. There was seldom a

125

courteous word spoken, and the poker was expert and cutthroat.

Mr. Newhouse was shuffling the cards expertly when a knock came on the corridor door.

Doc Breathit hit the table with the flat of his hand. "I knew it. Mrs. Jeffries' baby."

"Come in," Newhouse called.

The night clerk opened the door and stuck his head inside. "Somebody to see Miss Falette."

Isaac Maas looked at her. "So we bring sex into this."

Tess laughed and rose, as Breathit remarked dryly, "It's a woman's privilege to quit while she's ahead."

Tess made a face at him and walked out the door, closing it behind her.

Frank Chess was leaning against the wall. He shoved away from it, his slicker dripping water, and she could see that the rain had soaked his curly hair. His face was grim and unsmiling, lean and somehow haunted and beaten-looking.

"I've got to talk to you, Tess," Frank said. "Somewhere alone."

Tess said, "Come on," and walked past him up the corridor into the lobby. A half-dozen loafers were killing a rainy night in the lobby chairs, and Tess went on through to the empty dining room.

A wall lamp still burned in its bracket under a small table. Tess pulled a chair out and sat down, and Frank sat down across from her. He laid his soaking hat on the floor, and pulled his slicker open; his movements were swift and impatient, Tess noticed.

"Tess, have you got a key to the office at the lot?" Frank asked. When Tess nodded, Frank said quietly, "I'm in trouble; I need help, Tess."

She said nothing. Frank leaned forward and went on in a sober, quiet voice, "When did Rhino leave the lot tonight?"

"About five. He was headed for Saber. Didn't you see him?"

"No. I didn't come on the road. Who locked up, and when?"

"I did—a little after six."

"Were you alone?"

Tess nodded.

A wry grin came to Frank's face and went swiftly. He looked at her a silent, speculative moment, then said: "I was supposed to tell Rhino something at—no, I've got to prove I was in town at six tonight, Tess. I wasn't." He paused, and Tess said nothing, watching him, feeling a curious distaste for this.

"I was sent in to tell Rhino some things. If you could write out those things, I'll take your key and put the list on Rhino's desk tonight. Tomorrow, he'll ask about it, and you can tell him I came in at six, you wrote the message and left it on his desk."

He paused now, apparently seeing the reluctance in her face. Now he leaned over and said swiftly, earnestly, "It's important, Tess. I can't tell you how, only you've got to believe me."

Tess leaned back slowly in her chair and looked at him with pity in her eyes. She said, finally, "You can quit being afraid, Frank. He didn't die."

A startled look came into Frank's face now. He said cautiously, "Who didn't die?"

"Pete Faraday. You didn't kill him. He's hiding in the McGarritys' empty stable. I saw him, but too late to stop you signing over Saber." She leaned forward now and put her hand on his. "Frank," she said passionately, "get that look out of your eyes, now! Laugh once more! He's not dead! You've signed away half of Saber because you thought you killed him. Now, stand up and fight back at Rhino! It's over!"

Tess was expecting anything but what she saw now. An expression of black and bitter despair came into Frank's face then, and there was a dead hopelessness in his eyes. He only shook his head.

"Then that's not what you are afraid of?"

Again Frank shook his head in negation. He rose now and walked slowly across the dining room. Halfway across he paused, as if his mind was made up, and he came back to the table and leaned both hands on it and looked at her and said vehemently: "Tess, don't look at me that way any more! I'm doing what I have to do. Would it do any good if you knew some of it, some of the reasons why I have to do it?" His voice was low, deadly in earnest.

"If you want me to know," Tess said quietly.

"All right, I did a shady job for Rhino, a job that would lose me Carrie if she ever found it out." He paused, and then went on stubbornly, "She's the only kind and decent person I've known, and I've treated her badly. I'll do anything—*anything*

127

to keep from losing her. I've bought Rhino's silence with half of Saber. I'll buy it with all of it if I have to, just so I don't lose her! Now do you understand why I'm afraid?"

"No," Tess said bluntly. She started to rise, but Frank put a hand on her shoulder and pushed her down in the chair. They looked in each other's eyes for ten full seconds, and Tess's gaze did not falter.

"Say it," Frank said slowly.

"All right, you love Carrie. You want to live with her the rest of your life. But can you live with yourself the rest of that kind of life?"

Frank frowned. "What do you mean, Tess? Be plain."

"Where's the end to this blackmail? There isn't any. Are you going to cringe until you die? Nothing is worth that, Frank. Not even Carrie! Don't you see that?"

Frank straightened up, and his hands fell to his sides. His glance had never left her face. "If I tell her the truth, I lose her. I know that."

"Does she love you?"

"Yes."

"Then you won't lose her. You wouldn't lose me. You wouldn't lose any woman that's really a woman."

There was no belief in his face, she saw, and her heart was suddenly sick. She understood him now, understood his desperation and fear, and she pitied him more than she had ever pitied anybody—but she did not intend to let that pity alter her decision. She rose wearily, and this time he let her; she said in a voice, oddly without emotion: "No, Frank. I won't give you the key. I wouldn't, even if I knew what's behind your wanting it. I won't lie for you, either. If you can't tell her, you're already lost, and nothing will do any good."

She went past him now, and at the door she looked back at him. He was standing just as she had left him, looking at the table.

It was the clerk's footsteps pausing in the dining-room doorway that finally roused him minutes later. He reached down and picked up his hat and put it on, and then moved unseeing past the clerk through the lobby and outside. He paused here under the veranda beside the abandoned barrel chairs and automatically reached in his shirt pocket for his tobacco sack. It was sodden. He threw it into the gutter, and then stared at it, thinking, *It's come. I've fought it up to here, and this is the end of the road.* He moved out to the edge of the boardwalk and stared out into the wet night. Tess was right in one thing. Where was the end to this blackmail? There wasn't any end to it; he'd attempted the impossible. He might keep it from Carrie for months or for years, but sooner or later she'd find out. Tess's words came back to him: *Are you going to cringe until you die?* Yes, he'd even do that, if it would do any good. But it wouldn't, and he saw it now.

His horse jerked his head impatiently in the rain, and Frank glanced at him. Well, there was his horse, and there was the whole wide world before him. He could ride out quietly tonight and be out of this. Carrie would write him off then. A fiddlefoot, no good. It was a kinder judgment than the other, after all.

But he knew he wouldn't ride out. He'd come this far and he would go the rest of the way. She could hate him, but she couldn't say he'd dodged this. He untied his reins, ducked under the tie-rail, and stepped into the wet saddle.

The street was a mire of mud, and his horse splashed noisily as he turned him and headed up the street, toward Tavister's. In a little while now he would be hearing the words that he had been fearing to hear all along. That was as far as he would let himself think ahead.

He turned into Tavister's street, a kind of apathy in him. *Suppose Tess is right?* he thought. *Suppose she takes me anyway?* No, there was no use hoping; he'd been doping himself on too much of that lately, he thought wryly.

There were lamps lit in Tavister's house. He dismounted at the tie-rail, which was sheltered by the big pines in the yard, tied his horse and went up the walk and knocked on the door.

Carrie answered. When she saw who it was, she exclaimed, "You idiot, Frank! What are you doing out in this flood?"

"Waiting to be asked in."

Carrie pulled him inside and shut the door. She took one look at him and said, "The kitchen for you, son, with that slicker."

She headed for the kitchen and Frank fell in behind her. The dress she was wearing was one of his favorites—a long-sleeved maroon dress of flowered silk.

In the kitchen he shucked out of his slicker, tossed it into the sink, and then turned to look at Carrie. She was staring at him, and he looked down at his clothes. They were muddy and wet; one leg of his pants was torn from the scuffle with Albie.

Carrie said, "Well, a woman's work is never done on the day of a rain. Come on in and dirty up the parlor."

She waited until he came up to her, and she kissed him, and then she went on ahead. Frank followed her silently into the parlor. For the first time, it seemed, he was seeing the richness and the quiet elegance of this house. The rug was deep, the furniture black and polished. The overflow of books from the Judge's study lined a back wall. Carrie had been sitting in a big chair by the fire, mending. The log in the fireplace softly caved into the ashes now, and the flames stirred brightly.

Carrie went over to her chair and picked up one of the Judge's shirts. Frank thought, *This is my last look.* He went over to Carrie and took the mending from her hand and laid it in the sewing basket.

Carrie laughed, then, and put her head back against the chair. "Lord, I'm an old maid. I mend even when you're around."

Frank toed a footstool around in front of her chair and sat down facing her. He looked into the fire, and presently Carrie said, "You look tired, son."

He glanced at her and his smile died. Now was the time, but how was he to begin? He plunged. "Carrie, you were pretty proud of me taking in Rhino, weren't you?"

"I think he'll do you good."

"Want to know how I happened to take him in?"

Carrie nodded. Frank folded his hands between his knees and looked at them and began to talk.

"After that last row with Rob when I left Saber, I got work with Rhino. Know what I did for him?"

"Bought horses, didn't you?"

Frank still looked at his hands. "No. There were four of us— Hugh Nunnally, Pete Faraday and Albie Beecham and myself. Rhino had stolen an Army uniform somewhere. It fits me. It was the uniform of the cavalry, with the bars of a second lieutenant on it."

He looked up. She was listening, and his glance fell to his hands again. "I wore the uniform. I posed as Lieutenant Harding from Fort Garland. I was traveling through the country looking for cavalry mounts. You know, don't you, that the Army pays a hundred and twenty-five dollars for any horse that meets its standards?"

"That's good money for a horse, isn't it?" Carrie asked.

"Yes," Frank answered. He looked at her expectantly, waiting for the first sign of protest. There was none; she was listening carefully.

"I would go into a town alone, as Lieutenant Harding, and ask to see horses. The ranchers and the farmers would bring them in for me to see. Hugh Nunnally was always in the crowd that watched me look at horses. But I never bought any. I always rejected every horse showed me, but I had a code word when I rejected them. If I said the word 'sound' when I rejected the horse, Hugh always knew the horse was a good horse, that the Army would take it."

He looked up again. Carrie was watching him intently; she was understanding now.

He went on: "I disappointed a lot of ranchers and farmers. Sometimes they were pretty bitter when I rejected their horses. I was nice about it, but stubborn. I'd move on out of town. Hugh Nunnally would go up to the men who owned the horses I had rejected with the code word. He'd admire the horse, and start bargaining for it. He'd offer the standard price for a sound horse. That was forty dollars. Since the ranchers had just lost the chance to sell to the Army for a hundred and twenty-five dollars, they usually accepted Hugh's money."

Now he looked up again. He could see nothing but interest in Carrie's small face. What had he forgotten? He cast back, and he thought he'd said everything, but he went on doggedly: "Albie and Pete Faraday held the horses in one bunch in some safe canyon. When we had a bunch of them, we brought them back and Rhino sold them to the Army for a hundred and twenty-five dollars."

Now he waited, watching her face. She said then, "How very, very clever." There was no irony in her tone; she meant it.

He stared at her a long moment, then took a deep breath. "You don't understand," he said patiently. "I was wearing an Army uniform. I was impersonating an officer. That's a prison offense."

Carrie came alive then. She sat up straight and said, "Who knows it? You were never challenged, were you?"

Frank sat there, stunned. Carrie rose, at the look in his face, and he rose too. "Frank," she said swiftly. "Nunnally's not threatening to give you away?"

Frank said slowly: "You still don't understand. I was crooked. I swindled honest men out of the money rightly theirs by claiming to be an Army buyer."

"But that's horse-trading, isn't it?" Carrie asked. "You were just smarter than they were."

"You think so?" Frank asked slowly.

"Yes. Weren't you?"

Frank stood there for ten stupefied seconds, staring at her, until Carrie shook his arm. "Frank! What's the matter? Why are you looking at me like that?"

He turned then, without a word, and walked out into the kitchen. He shrugged into his slicker, picked up his sodden hat, and came back into the hall, where Carrie was waiting for him.

He stopped before her, feeling the torrent of words welling up in him, gathering like an avalanche, and running through his mind like some idiot refrain was the thought, *She hasn't forgiven me because she doesn't even know I've done wrong.*

"Frank," Carrie said tartly, "what's got into you? Where are you going? What's the *matter* with you?"

Frank shook his head, and rubbed the back of his neck slowly with the palm of his hand. "I've got to get some sleep," he said gently. "Good night, Carrie." He brushed past her and went out.

He was halfway down the walk when he heard her calling, "Frank, come back! Frank!"

He didn't answer. Mounting his horse, he rode back the way he had come. There was a kind of numbness in his mind. It refused to think, and all he knew was that he had not lied to Carrie when he said he had to have sleep. He thought of the hotel, and rejected that. He might see Tess, and he didn't want to face her now.

The McGarritys' rooms were empty. He headed for them and at the small woodshed in the rear of the building, which the McGarritys were using for a stable, he dismounted. There was a horse inside already. Frank shoved him over, moved his horse in beside him, and then tramped up the stairs in the darkness.

He opened the door and stepped inside and called, "John?"

A sleepy voice said, "Who is it?" from the back room.

"Frank. I want a place to sleep."

"Help yourself," John answered sleepily.

Frank went into the dark front room. He didn't bother to light the lamp, but stripped off his wet clothes and crawled under the blankets of Jonas's bed. Lying there listening to the rain on the roof, he thought it might be slacking off.

He thought of Carrie now, and in his mind there was a quality of unbelief in the happenings of this evening. But they were true. She didn't think he'd done wrong. He had broken with Rhino and threatened him, he had hidden Rob's killer, he had submitted to loss of half of Saber, he had lied a hundred times, he had almost been murdered today, he was partners with a horse thief, he had been blackmailed twice over, and he had cringed—all to keep from Carrie the fact he had been a swindler. And now she knew, she didn't think he'd done wrong.

He laughed aloud then, the irony of it coming to him.

He heard John's footsteps in the hall, and then they paused in the doorway.

"What's so damn funny, Frank? You drunk?"

"No. You wouldn't understand." He lay there, smiling in the darkness, then he came up on one elbow. "John, send a man tomorrow to bring back your horses. You're in business again."

There was a long silence, then John moved across the room. He came over to the bed, and struck a match, holding it over his head. Frank blinked against its sudden light. John was standing there in his baggy underwear, his sparse hair awry, his toes curling away from the cold floorboards. But his round face was deadly serious.

"That's nothing to joke about," he said slowly.

"I'm not joking. Send him."

"What about Rhino?"

Frank rolled over on his back and looked up at the ceiling. "He'll be in jail tomorrow. So will Nunnally." He hesitated a moment. "So will I. Now get to bed, will you?"

Chapter 18

WHEN BUCK HANNAN STEPPED OUT of the Colorado House after a solid breakfast, there were only a couple of loafers in the barrel chairs on the veranda. Buck said, "Beautiful mornin', boys," and walked out into the bright sunlight on the edge of the boardwalk. The air was heavy with the rich smell of sun on soaked earth. He sniffed it appreciatively before he fired up a thick cigar, and then he contemplated the road. One wagon had been out already and left twin gashes in the muddy street. The pools of water had shrunk, but Buck knew the mud was soft, and he swore crossly. Somebody ought to plank these crossings so a man could go more than a block and still be dryshod, he thought.

Resignedly, he stepped into the mud and hurriedly negotiated the cross-street. It was just a matter of time, anyway, before his boots were muddy. He had to ride out to Dutra's on business about Rob's death this morning, and there'd still be mud aplenty. At the thought of how little he knew of Rob's killer, how little he had done or could do about it, he scowled.

He spoke affably to the few passers-by he met, and was soon at the cinder path at the edge of town. When he came to Hulst's horse lot, he looked at the great pool of water under the gate and swore again.

Skirting it widely and coming around from the other side, he managed to achieve the office steps and loading platform without getting his boots soaked, and he was pleased and in a good humor again.

He poked his head in the office, and saw Tess Falette and Shinner just opening the safe. Buck said, "Mornin', Tess."

She said good morning and smiled sweetly at him, and he said from the door, "Tell me, honest-to-God, Tess, did you really fill in that last straight?"

"You wouldn't pay to find out," Tess reminded him.

134

"I'm curious. Tell me."

"Get a warrant."

Buck grinned and went on down the loading platform. There was a beautiful girl, he thought, and he winced a little when he remembered last night. He should have stuck to his usual game of playing the percentages, but playing with a woman it was different. You had to play hunch poker with them out of self-defense—or at least he'd thought so until last night.

He went back toward the stables, and a hostler said, "Mornin', Sheriff."

"Mornin'," Buck said. "Get my horse for me, will you? Big Black."

"Sure, I know him." The man went off to the stable and Buck loitered along behind him. He hauled up in the sun outside the stable, and let its warmth soak into him. The hostler came to the stable door in a moment and shouted, "Bud, where's the sheriff's horse?"

Someone across the lot yelled, "He's in there."

Then a wrangle started, and a couple of men drifted across to the stable. Buck smoked contentedly. He paid no attention as the three men came out, glancing obliquely at him, and went over toward the corrals. Presently, however, he became impatient. He walked to the corner of a corral and looked down the drive. He saw a half-dozen men gathered in a group talking, and among them was his hostler.

As he started for them, he saw them look at him, and then they spread out, waiting for him.

"Find him?" Buck asked pleasantly of his hostler.

"He ain't there," the man blurted out. "He ain't anywhere on the lot."

Buck snorted. "Look again."

They scattered. In five minutes they were back again. The sheriff's horse wasn't here.

"Go get Nunnally," Buck said, in disgust. Nunnally wasn't there, they said. Neither was Rhino. Buck felt his temper rising a little, and he looked carefully at them and said, "Which one of you wanted to show off to your girl? In the rain, too. Who rode him?"

135

"He was in that corral at nine last night," a man said, pointing to the stable corral. "I forked him some hay."

A faint apprehension came to Hannan then. The man who had just spoken said to his companion, "You drove 'em to water this mornin', Hodge. Was he there?"

"Now I remember, no," the man said emphatically.

Buck, trailed by every hostler on the lot now, walked over to the stable and looked inside. He felt foolish after he got there; the horse wouldn't materialize out of thin air. He dropped his cigar now and said: "You mean, somebody could steal a horse out of here? Don't you lock the stables? Isn't there a night watchman around?"

The crew looked at each other and shifted their feet uneasily. "Somebody's always sleepin' in the barn," someone volunteered.

Buck felt his neck getting hot. He had hold of the other end of the stick, now. There was nobody to report a stolen horse to except himself. And the fact that his, the sheriff's, horse was stolen, was outrageous. Nobody stole a sheriff's horse; it was tantamount to committing suicide, and the whole world knew it. He couldn't conceive of anybody with the idiocy—or the gall—to do it, yet the horse was gone. Taken out of a public lot.

He said now, "A couple of you go out on the road, and shove everything that comes by off it. Keep it clear for tracks."

He tramped out of the stable and halted. If anybody was laughing at him, daring him to make something of this, he'd take the dare, and damn quick. *You're gettin' redheaded,* he told himself. He took a deep breath and looked at the rear gate of the lot near-by, thinking closely now. There was one thing important to know, and that was whether the horse had been taken while it was raining, or after the rain had stopped.

The drive through the rear gate was trampled heavily. Outside the fence, Buck turned downriver, but he gave that up immediately. Nothing but a pair of dogs had been along here since the rain, the dirt showed.

He turned upriver, and immediately, once he was clear of the tracks of the horses who were driven down to water this morning, he saw the tracks of a horse. There were boot tracks, too, clear, and they had been made since the rain. He followed them over to a tree, where there were the tracks of another horse. Simple enough: the thief had simply led the black to his waiting horse, mounted, and led the black off.

The hostlers watched him in silence. Buck found a clear set of tracks where the trees hadn't dripped water on them, and knelt, examining the tracks. A glance told him it was his black. The left hind foot toed in, and the frog of its shoe was distinctive. The tracks were about five hours old, he judged. He rose and eyed the tracks as they continued upriver, plain in the clean-washed clay of the wagon road. A slow and solid wrath stirred again in him.

He said to the men, "Saddle me a horse, a good stayer, and be quick about it."

When the horse was brought him, he mounted and set out parallel to the tracks. At the cross-street by McGarrity's freight yard, they turned and Buck turned with them. They crossed the main street, and then were mingled with the tracks of other horses, but the traffic had been light so far this morning and Buck had no trouble following them to the base of the hill.

Reining up here, he considered. Putting aside his own personal feelings, the insult to him, what was the best thing to do? Anybody fool enough to steal a sheriff's horse was fool enough to wait in the brush and shoot the sheriff when he came after the horse. Then, too, with a five-hour start, the thief might be headed out of the country, which meant long riding. If the thief took to the trails, there were ways to block him. Everything pointed, Hannan decided, to the necessity for several men. He accepted this reluctantly, with a wry foreknowledge of the grins it would bring.

Accordingly, he rode back to the main street. He was undecided about the best place to raise some deputies, but he'd start with the Pleasant Hour.

A scattering of horses at the tie-rail told him there were riders here. He didn't much like the idea of depending on men who opened saloons in the morning, but there was no choice. As he dismounted, he looked over the brands of the horses and saw several Saber brands. That was different. The old Saber crew had been replaced by Rhino's men and this was only a loafing place for them until another job turned up. They weren't saloon bums.

He went inside and tramped back through the room, sizing up the scattering of men here. He saw old Cass Hardesty sitting at the idle monte table, his stubby pipe fuming; Cass was wearing a pair of iron-rimmed glasses, studying a crumpled week-old paper. He looked as if he'd read it five times already.

Buck went up to him and said, "Want to catch a horse thief, Cass, on deputy's pay?"

"If it'll get me out of here," Cass said.

"Any of your old bunch around?"

"Johnny Samuels, Pete Hargis, Joe Rich."

"Round 'em up," Buck said briefly.

Ten minutes later, Hannan, with his four deputies, was at the base of the hill examining the tracks.

"Whose horse?" Cass said.

"Mine."

Cass smiled faintly under his mustache. "There's a hero."

The traveling, once they were on top of the hill, was good. The tracks were absurdly easy to follow; there had been no pretense made at covering them. They clung to the Wells Canyon road on the way to the pass for some miles, and then struck off on a side trail traveling east, when the tracks turned off. They stopped here to blow their horses.

"He'll get some hard goin' over there," Johnny Samuels observed looking toward the east.

Single file, they took to the trail, Hannan ahead. He soon saw that the rider ahead knew his way around the country. He kept working east, choosing the right trails, crossing Horn Creek into the Saber range. Once, they saw where he had stopped and shifted saddles to Hannan's horse. Buck dismounted here and looked at the tracks, crumbling the side of them with his finger to test the consistency of the mud.

"We're close," he said.

Later, at a fork in the trails, they saw where two riders, coming from the south, joined up with the lone rider. The three of them kept east.

Buck moved more cautiously now, dropping three of his men back so they would not all walk into an ambush. Presently, Buck came out on a timbered ridge, and he reined in so abruptly that Cass's horse, following, bumped his. Cass pulled up alongside and Buck pointed.

The ridge broke for a little park, and Cass first saw Hannan's big black horse picketed out in the grass of the clearing. There were three other horses with it. Off to the right in the shade of the fringing timber, Cass could make out the shape of three men lounging around a small fire.

Buck turned back and he and Cass waited for the others to come up. When they were all assembled, Buck gave them a description of the park, and told them his plan. Dismounted, the four of them would work around through the timber until they were on every side of the camp. After twenty minutes had passed, he would ride down the trail into the camp. A single man wouldn't alarm them. If trouble broke, Cass was to stampede their horses, and then they would have the rustlers.

Alone now, Buck felt a grim pleasure. There were several things that didn't seem quite right about this, though, the main one being that the thief hadn't even attempted to cover his tracks and he could have easily. Another was that the three of them were heading into the high country around the peaks to the east, where they could be easily cornered.

When the twenty minutes were past, Buck mounted, and rode on up to the ridge and took the trail down it. Once on the flats, he saw one of the men at the fire rise, and Buck's hand fell to his gun. He rode stolidly on, in not much of a hurry, and when he got closer he pulled his gun and held it at his side.

When he recognized the man standing, he let out a soft expletive, and pushed his horse on into the camp and reined up.

It was Frank Chess standing there. Sitting around the fire were the McGarrity brothers.

Buck said, "Was it you, Frank?"

Frank nodded, and at sight of Frank's face, handsome, tired, but with a veiled friendliness in it, Buck's wrath rose like a brush fire.

"Damn you, Chess, you *want* to hang, don't you?"

Chapter 19

Jonas McGarrity said dryly, "Get it off your chest, Buck, and then listen to him."

Others were drifting into camp now, Frank saw. He counted four of them, all old Saber hands, among them Cass. None of them spoke to him. Cass, when he saw him, took the pipe out of his mouth long enough to spit contemptuously. Joe Rich's grin was full of malice, and he didn't blame him. Johnny Samuels looked at him as if he had thought all along that a horse thief's end was long overdue.

But it was Hannan who was really angry. Frank waited to see if Buck would take Jonas's advice. Hannan, however, didn't speak for a moment, and then he looked at the McGarritys and said in a hard voice, "I can understand Frank. But you two."

Frank said mildly, "Have any trouble following me, Buck?"

"No, you bungled that, like the rest of it."

"Maybe on purpose. Maybe he wanted you to follow him," Jonas McGarrity suggested.

"Why?" Hannan snarled.

Frank asked, "Buck, if I'd stopped you on the street last night and told you Rhino Hulst had a hundred stolen horses cached back in the hills, what would you have done?"

"Called you a liar," Hannan said promptly.

"If I'd asked you to come out and see for yourself, would you have done it?"

"No."

Frank said unsmilingly, "That's why I stole your horse."

Hannan's face lost some of its anger. The man was no fool, and he was fair, Frank knew, once a man got past his temper. Buck asked, "So you stole him to get me up here?"

Frank nodded. "Without your first going to Rhino or Hugh about it. I hoped you'd bring along some others, and you did."

Buck stepped heavily out of the saddle. Frank saw Cass

glance quizzically at Johnny Samuels. Buck came forward now to face Frank. "Well, I'm here."

"You'll go?"

"Hell, I got to. Any man that would steal a sheriff's horse to get him to look at something must mean it. He better mean it."

Frank told him then of what he had seen yesterday, from his early break from Saber through his meeting with Hugh to seeing the horses driven in at dusk and Albie's threat to kill him and the subsequent fight. As he talked, the old Saber hands moved closer to listen, and Hannan paid him a close attention. When he was finished, Hannan looked at him searchingly.

"Rhino is your partner, isn't he?"

"All right."

"What do you mean, 'all right'?" Hannan said truculently. "For all I know, you're in it together—if it's true. Or you've fought—if it's true—and you're turning him up. Or he squeezed you out and you're sore."

"One thing at a time, Buck," Frank said patiently. "Get your proof, then you can take me with them if you want."

Hannan gave him a strange, wondering look before he said, "Lead off, then."

They saddled up, and Johnny Samuels took Hannan's horse and went back for their mounts. Once they were assembled, Frank led off down the trail.

He at least had Hannan's presence, and he had the help of seven men, and now he would play it through any way he had to, just so long as Rhino and Nunnally were broken. After that, the rest of it would come and he would take his medicine. There was no use pretending to himself he didn't mind, because he did. But that grinding fear, coupled with the bleak despair that had been riding him these weeks, was gone now. The worse that could or would happen was better than that, and he felt strangely cheerful.

They came to the edge of the wild canyon country in early afternoon, and Frank reckoned they were north of the corral. There were no trails here, and he plunged into the first gully with nothing more than a vague feeling of the canyon's location to guide him.

It was steaming hot in these airless, wet, brush-choked washes, and at times it seemed that they were aimlessly floundering up one ridge and down another, but presently, after more than an hour of it, Frank came to a campsite from years past. It was so old that the stumps where they had cut wood were grayed over, but he knew now that over the next ridge, they would be in the wash that passed the corral. He reined up and passed the word back to Cass, who passed it on.

He and Cass glanced at each other briefly then, and their glances fell away. There was only one way to prove to Cass, and the others, that he was not the renegade to Saber and himself they thought him, and that was by uncovering Rhino. Words were of no use now and he didn't attempt them.

Hannan came crashing through the brush then and reined up. His shirt was soaked with sweat, and his face red and scratched by the brush. Frank told him where they were.

"Think he'll have some of the crew there?" Hannan asked.

Frank shook his head in negation and told him his belief. The three riders who drove the stolen bunch yesterday were being followed reasonably close, else they would not have been so eager to get the tracks blotted immediately. Now that the horses were fenced tightly and had plenty of grass and water, and all tracks into the canyon rained out, Nunnally would keep his crew away from it until danger was past.

Hannan accepted this without objection. He put his horse ahead of Frank and led off, climbing the next ridge, and slipping and skidding his horse down its far side into the wash. Turning down it, they presently came to the spread in the wash, and ahead of them Frank saw the canyon. But he could not see the fence, and for a moment his heart sank. And then he saw that Hugh's crew had cut brush and stacked it in front of the fence to hide it.

He dropped out of line now and rode over to the brush, and Hannan halted, watching him suspiciously. Frank leaned out of the saddle and yanked a section of the brush away, revealing the new-cut poles of the fence. The rough gate was wired shut, and he swung it open, and again Hannan led the way. A quarter-mile up the canyon, they rounded a bend and saw the first horses, and Frank relaxed in the saddle. Riding on, nobody said anything, and they came to a bigger bunch.

These horses raised their heads and looked at them without curiosity, and went back to their grazing.

"Recognize any brands?" Hannan asked.

Frank rode among them and came back, and told Hannan there were two Utah brands he recognized. The others were new to him.

Hannan sat in the saddle a long moment, looking at the horses, and then he remarked, "For all I know, Rhino may have the bill of sale for every horse in this canyon."

Cass Hardesty said dryly: "Don't be so bullheaded, Buck. There's that fence he tried to cover up. Take Frank's word."

Hannan looked over at Cass. "I'll ask you. What do you think his word is worth?"

The gibe hit home, Frank saw. His word to Cass and the others hadn't been worth anything. Hannan sat there lost in thought, while the others watched him, and Frank could guess what was going through his mind. Rhino and Nunnally were widely respected men; Frank Chess was known to be unreliable. A blunder here would be serious, and this was a time for caution. Frank guessed shrewdly that the proof Hannan demanded and which now lay before him set up a barrier to further action. The very size of the theft demanded careful collection of proof, and Hannan, a fair man, was capable of going back to town, disbanding this group, and begin his careful collection of that proof. The scales must be tipped so that Hannan would act now, Frank knew, and now he knew also he must gamble.

"That's a pretty serious charge against Rhino, isn't it, Buck?"

Hannan looked at him carefully. "They hang a man for stealing *one* horse."

"Then go back to town and think it over. Give him time to alter the brands and forge bills of sale, or even get rid of the horses. You can still go at him from another direction." Frank's tone was dry, thrusting, purposely so.

Hannan's temper rose like a flag. "What direction?"

"Why, he murdered Rob."

The statement fell like a stone dropped into a pool. There was a ripple of movement among these men, looks exchanged between them, and afterward utter silence. Hannan's level gaze never left Frank's face, and there was a long and un-broken silence.

Frank said then with a wicked sarcasm: "Write him a letter, Buck. Then you won't have to see him."

It didn't work. Hannan said quietly, "What are you tryin' to make me do?"

"Move," Frank said sharply. "Rhino's at Saber. So's Hugh. Go in and brace them. If I'm lying, you can still hang me."

Without another word, Hannan pulled his horse around and started down canyon. At its mouth and through the fence, he said to Frank, "Get us out of here."

"Where do you want to go?"

"Saber."

Chapter 20

FULL DARKNESS caught them still in the crescent meadows above Saber. Hannan talked of many things, and not once did he mention Rob. But Frank knew the accounting would come at Saber, and that Hannan would be merciless with him. Hannan wanted to know the habits of the crew there at this time of the evening, and Frank couldn't tell him. However, they agreed it seemed reasonable that if Rhino was there, he and Hugh would be in the big house, away from the crew in the bunkhouse.

Accordingly, Hannan made his careful disposition of the men. If there was a light in the office, they would skirt the wagon shed and place themselves between the bunkhouse and the house. He and Frank would tackle Rhino and Hugh in the office. Nobody was to disturb them, nobody was to leave.

Afterward, they were silent. The jingle of the bridle chains and the stretching creak of saddle leather was a pleasant sound in the night, and Frank found himself speculating, without caring much, what the next hour would bring. Hannan was here; Hannan would see it all and hear it all, and that was the important thing. Last night in Jonas' room, after he knew he was going to kill Rhino, he saw that any way he reasoned it, Hannan must be there to see it and hear it. And he had seen some of it already, the stolen horses and the scene of his fight with Albie.

The lights of Saber showed now, and Frank watched the house until the dim glow of the office window was visible. On the damp turf, their horses made little sound. Skirting the wagon shed, one of the horses blundered into a discarded grindstone, and raised a racket, but nobody appeared immediately in the bunkhouse doorway.

The sound of the horses, however, as they cut between the bunkhouse and the house, brought a couple of hands to the bunkhouse door.

Hannan called to them, "Take it easy, boys. Just stay there."

Frank was watching the office door as he dismounted. Now it opened and Hugh Nunnally's broad figure was framed in it. He put a shoulder against the door frame and called pleasantly, "Who is it?"

"Buck, Hugh," Hannan answered.

Frank fell in beside him and they tramped over to the doorway. Inside, Frank saw Rhino tilted back in Jess Irby's chair, fingers laced across the top of his white hair.

When Hugh saw Frank, he straightened slowly. The light was behind Hugh, so that Frank could not see his face. Frank said, "Hello, Hugh," in a mild, dry voice.

Hugh turned then and said over his shoulder to Rhino, "Buck picked him up, Rhino." He stepped aside then, and said, "Come in."

Buck went in first. As Frank passed Hugh, he saw the hard uncertainty in Hugh's eyes, and Hugh reached out to lift the gun from his holster.

Frank wheeled away from him into the room, and said, "Hunhunh."

Hugh glanced protestingly at Buck. "He's packin' a gun, Buck."

"What of it? I've got a bunch out here," Hannan said. Hannan was shrewdly playing up to the lead Hugh had given him, Frank saw. Buck walked over to the leather sofa and sat down.

Rhino had a toothpick in the corner of his mouth. He waved it idly at Buck in greeting and then looked at Frank. There was no concern in Rhino's eyes.

"What I'd like to know is what happened?" Hannan said. He was fishing for information, Frank saw, with a bland gall. Nunnally closed the door and drifted across the room to the edge of the desk. A wary alertness was in his eyes, and Frank knew he was wondering what was shaping up.

Rhino took the toothpick from his mouth. "He killed Albie. Frank shot at him last week, when they were drivin' a bunch of horses over to Crawford. When Albie saw him yesterday, he called Frank on it. Frank shot him. Albie didn't have a gun, so he didn't have a chance."

"Where was this?"

Rhino tilted his head. "In the bunkhouse."

That was the first lie, and Frank saw Hannan's jaw set a little. Hannan said, "He says he shot him up by the Elk Creek corral."

"Why does he want to lie about it?" Rhino asked wonderingly.

"He didn't. I saw where they scuffled. There was still some blood there under the leaves."

Frank saw Nunnally's back straighten. Hannan at the Elk Creek corral was trouble.

Nunnally's tone was lazy and not even curious as he asked now, "What were you doing up there, Frank?"

"Watching a bunch of horses come in from over the peaks."

The warning in Nunnally's eyes was hard and instantaneous. "Lister's bunch from the lot," he murmured.

"Another bunch," Frank said gently. "Lister's bunch went up to cover their tracks."

Rhino asked mildly, "What are you trying to say, Frank?" and Frank's gaze shifted to him. Rhino's face was bland and untroubled, but Frank saw the faint perspiration beginning to bead his forehead and he knew he had him.

"That three riders—I think they're in the bunkhouse now—drove a bunch of horses off the peaks, through the meadow, and back to the corral Hugh and your crew were finishing. That Lister used your horses from the lot to cover their tracks."

"Rot," Rhino snorted.

"I saw them," Hannan said calmly.

There was a thin and tenuous silence for a few seconds, and Frank pushed away from the wall. Now he said wickedly, looking at Rhino: "I've already told Carrie about the uniform, Rhino. She doesn't care. Now tell Hannan about Rob."

Ponderously, Rhino tilted forward in his swivel chair, his body coming between Frank and Nunnally. And Hugh, seeing he was protected, reached down with his right hand, palmed open the corridor door, and lunged through it into the corridor.

Frank's gun came up and he drove for the door Rhino's chair was blocking. Out of the corner of his eyes, he saw Hannan's gun come out. He crashed into Rhino, knocking him back in the chair, and the drive of his body and Rhino's weight sent the chair over backwards. The impact of Rhino's fall shook the room. The lamp on the desk tilted, fell, and went out.

Wrenching the door open, Frank heard Hannan's still mild voice say, "Get him, boy," and he plunged through the door, a wicked elation in him. Hugh's gun bellowed from the living room, and Frank heard the slug hit the wall behind him. Nunnally had been waiting there with drawn gun for the first fool to follow him and be framed in the lamplight. Only Rhino's fall had tipped the lamp.

Frank crouched and moved cautiously ahead, and now he called, "Careful of that sofa, Hugh."

But Nunnally was not to be baited into speaking if he was in the room. Now an unholy racket of shots came from outside, as the crew in the bunkhouse, hearing Hugh's shot, opened up. Strangely, as Frank waited there, trying to hear Hugh's movements, he heard the low, conversational voices of Rhino and Hannan talking.

He inched ahead now into the room and knelt, listening. Not a sound. Nunnally was waiting somewhere in the house, the same as he was, for a sound to shoot at. He opened his mouth and breathed through it and was utterly still listening. This was a fool's game, he knew beyond thought. Nunnally was in another room already, but the house was surrounded, and he would fight till he was killed. Why follow him? He

147

had moved upstairs, or to another room, and there were a thousand places he could hide, waiting to put a bullet into whoever followed him.

But a hot and stubborn anger held Frank where he was. Nunnally was his, and his alone, and he would not turn back.

And then the thought came to him, *What if he doesn't know the house?* Hugh had been here only a few days, and he'd been grimly busy. He wouldn't care enough about the house to look at it. Then if he didn't know the house, and the placement of the furniture, he would be too wise to blunder around in the dark. *Then he'll be here, in this room,* Frank thought. A faint chill touched his back when he considered that.

The firing outside continued. Here, there was an unrelieved blackness that seemed to breathe all around him. He knew now that he had to move, to end this tension that was building here. Remembering the room now, he took a quiet step to his left and then felt slowly with his hand. It touched a table. Gently, gently, he moved it, and presently his hand touched the lamp. He stopped, remembering this lamp. It was the plain one, not the one with the glass-bead fringe.

He grasped it firmly around the base and waited. It was silent outside. He wanted the sound of gunfire to cover what he would do next.

Suddenly, there was a crash of gunfire just outside the room. Frank lifted the lamp and silently heaved it across the room now. Its crash against the far wall was hard and brittle and startling. Instantaneously, only five feet to his right, Hugh's gun opened up in the direction of the lamp's crash. Frank pivoted and shot three times, waist-high, pulling his gun in a tight arc.

And then he moved forward swiftly.

He crashed into Hugh's body, which was turned to him. Frank slashed out with his gun, raking it across Hugh's face, and he heard the grunt, and Hugh's arm came down across his shoulder like an axe. Then there was a deafening roar behind him, as Hugh's gun went off in his hand.

Frank rolled away from the arm and drove his left hand into Hugh's midriff, as he was brought up abruptly by the wall. His fist smacked solidly in Hugh's belly, and then skidded wetly off. Frank raised his gun and hacked down savagely at Hugh's head, but his gun met nothing, and he was carried off balance.

And then the thudding crash of Hugh falling on the floor followed. Frank fell into a tangle of legs and he clawed up onto Hugh's body, slashing again with his gun. But Nunnally did not move under him.

Frank rolled away and waited. He heard a thin sigh, and that was all.

Now he rose, fumbling for a match with his left hand in his shirt pocket while he held his gun ready with the other hand. His hand was set. Cautiously, he circled around Hugh's head and wiped the match alight on the wall.

There at his feet, lying on his back, with open eyes and arms outstretched, was Nunnally. A great ragged gash angled down his face. The whole front of his shirt was stained with blood. Slowly, Frank raised his own left hand and saw the blood on his fist, and he knew that Nunnally had been dead on his feet when he hit him.

The match died, and he moved around Hugh and felt his way into the corridor. A wavering light showed under the door, and when Frank palmed it open he saw Hannan kneeling in the outside doorway, holding a match. There, lying on the steps, one tremendous leg in the room, was Rhino. He was face down.

Frank walked across the room and Hannan rose. There were two bullet holes in Rhino's back, and the stains from them had merged to soak his shirt.

Hannan looked at Frank blankly. "The damn fool ran. I had a gun on him, and he tried to break."

"So you'll never know about Rob?" Frank said bitterly.

"Why, he told me all about it," Hannan said wonderingly. "Faraday did it and Rhino paid him. That's why I thought he'd quit. I thought he'd given up." He looked down at the massive, still form of the gray-haired man at his feet. The firing at the bunkhouse had ceased, and it was quiet now, and still Hannan looked at Rhino. "You know," he said then, "I'm a sucker. That's just what Rhino wanted me to do."

They rode into town next day about noon, four of Rhino's disarmed crew riding ahead. Two of the crew lay dead by the corrals at Saber, and the rest had made a successful break for the hills. The four were Hannan's loot, and he seemed satisfied.

As they swung into the main street, Frank asked, "Where'll you be, Buck?"

"At the hotel, I reckon. Why?"

Frank only said, "I'll see you later," and fell away from the group and turned up the side street toward Tavister's house.

Now he slowed his horse to a walk, and looked up the quiet tree-shaded street to the big brick house. It was all the way he pictured it last night as he lay in his room, only last night he hadn't gone beyond here. In his mind, he had turned up the side street, and the rest of it wouldn't come.

He saw Carrie in the porch chair as he reined up at the stepping block. He swung out of the saddle now, and tied his horse, and then moved through the iron gate up the walk.

Carrie had put her book down, and now she rose and came to the top of the steps. She was wearing his favorite dress, he saw, and before he glanced up to her face he thought, *She's pretty in it,* and then he looked closely at her.

She knows it, he thought then. She didn't say anything, although her face was tight and unsmiling as he came onto the bottom step and halted. Her arm was around the porch pillar, and for a moment they just looked at each other, neither offering to move closer.

"I don't know how to begin it," Frank said then.

"It wasn't fair, Frank," Carrie said bitterly.

"I didn't know any other way to do it," Frank said humbly. "You see, I'd run out my rope, Carrie. I'd lied to you, I'd lied to everybody. I'd given Rhino half of Saber to keep it from you, and I still couldn't keep it from you, so I had to tell you."

"And I still don't care if you did it," Carrie said.

"No, you care about me being steady, and staying put, and owning something big. You care enough about that to wait six years to see if I'll do it, don't you, Carrie?"

She didn't answer.

"Don't wait any more," Frank said gently. Still she didn't say anything, and he turned and went down the walk and through the gate to his horse. She wouldn't call him back, he knew. He mounted and put his horse in motion and glanced over at the porch. She hadn't moved, and he looked away.

He went down to the main street which was almost empty at noon hour, and he saw the horses out in front of McGarritys' gate, where Hannan and his men were gathering in Pete Faraday. There weren't any people standing around watching, so he knew the news wasn't out yet.

He put his horse in at the tie-rail of the hotel, and walked around the rail and into the lobby, crossing it to the dining-room door.

When he saw Tess there, he took off his hat and went over to her table, where she was eating with Mr. Newhouse.

He grinned down at her and said, "You've had enough to eat. Come along."

She smiled and rose, not even excusing herself, and he held her hand as they walked through the dining room and lobby.

Outside, she said, "You look different."

"I am different," he said. They turned down the cross street toward McGarrity's. The Saber crew and Faraday were mounting now, and Frank, still holding her hand, stopped and waited as they passed him, Faraday riding sullenly amongst them.

Cass said, "Hello, Boss."

Frank grinned, and now he saw Hannan walking toward the hotel, leading his horse. He was mopping his brow with a soiled handkerchief as he came up to them, and he touched his hat to Tess, his handkerchief still in his hand.

Frank looked down at Tess, and then glanced at Hannan. "Buck, I'm not scared any more. You want me, along with those four and Faraday, for impersonating an Army officer."

He felt Tess's hand squeeze his.

Buck said mildly, "I wondered when you were goin' to tell me."

"You knew it?" Frank said blankly.

"Yeah. Rhino told me last night." He looked closely at Frank. "I think he's a liar."

"No, he didn't lie." He told Hannan then how he and Nunnally had worked it, and Hannan listened with an increasing irritation.

When he was finished, Hannan said, "What do you want me to do about it?"

"Whatever's in the book."

Hannan looked at him, and then at Tess, and he snorted, "I haven't heard the Army kick." When Frank didn't answer, Hannan just shook his head, touched his hat and walked on.

Frank turned to Tess, bewilderment in his face.

"Maybe he thinks you've paid enough," Tess said gravely.

"Do *you* think it was wrong?" Frank asked.

"Yes."

"Tess," Frank said slowly, "I'm a fiddlefoot. I don't want Saber for a while. I want to see some country, Utah first. I want to take five thousand dollars, my own, and go through those Utah towns with Rhino's bills of sale for those horses. I want to hunt up those men and pay them what I owe them." He paused, "I want you with me. I want to marry you. I—"

"Haven't you something else to do first?"

"I've done that. I told her."

She smiled proudly then, and she said, without shyness, "I think I'm really a fiddlefoot, too."

They turned then, walking contentedly back toward the hotel, and it was a minute before Frank spoke. Then he said, with a gay and veiled derision in his voice: "First, though, I'm going fishing. Up in Wells Canyon there's a big trout as long as my arm. He's been there six years, the same pool. Fat, dumb, and happy. I'm going to catch him."